MORNINGTON CRESCENT

MORNINGTON CRESCENT

by

Vivian Roberts

Dales Large Print Books
Long Preston, North Yorkshire,
BD23 4ND, England.

British Library Cataloguing in Publication Data.

Roberts, Vivian
    Mornington Crescent.

    A catalogue record of this book is
    available from the British Library

    ISBN   978-1-84262-767-9 pbk

Copyright © Working Partners Two 2009

Cover illustration © Martin Amis by arrangement with
Arcangel Images

The moral right of the author has been asserted

Published in Large Print 2010 by arrangement with
Working Partners Two

Dales Large Print is an imprint of Library Magna Books Ltd.

Printed and bound in Great Britain by
T.J. (International) Ltd., Cornwall, PL28 8RW

With Special Thanks to Jean Davidson

For Juliet and Penny, with love

1

Walking towards the Lost Property Office, Natalia O'Shea pushed a limp strand of fine, pale-brown hair back from her face, her skin already feeling damp and sticky to the touch. She didn't know if this was global warming or not, but she did know that London, like any big city in a heat wave, was not a comfortable place to be. Back down in the Underground, she'd practically had to peel herself from some businessman squashed against her.

Stepping out into the morning light, Baker Street was a profusion of colours as Londoners shed their winter blacks, browns and greys. Women and girls wore skimpy dresses, or skirts and tops in bold prints, or white cotton and natural linen. Men wore loose shirts in pastel colours, and many had abandoned trousers for khaki, knee-length shorts, and the distinctively English ensemble of sandals and socks. When the shove came, it took her unprepared, the man cannoning into her out of nowhere.

Natalia felt his elbow hard against her upper arm, the weight of his body pushing her off balance. As she struggled to stay upright, she caught the smell of stale body odour as her assailant turned to face her. Looking up sharply, she totally expected to stare into the black eyes of her ex-husband, Jem. She'd been half-dreading, half-hoping that this might happen for months, ever since she'd learned he was in the country. With their son, Paul.

Instead, hard, pale-blue eyes met hers. She could see droplets of sweat running down from his shaven head. Then she heard a reassuring London voice.

'Sorry, love. You all right? Don't know I'm born, me.'

The man barely waited to see her nod, then was gone, barrelling on down Baker Street towards the Marylebone Road.

Yards from the office now, heart thumping, Natalia took a deep breath and almost choked. Even though it was barely nine o'clock in the morning, the air was hot and dry, tangy with the acrid fumes of diesel and petrol exhausts from the cars, buses, lorries, taxis and motorbikes that formed a solid mass in the street; the usual rush-hour traffic jam. In the still, hot air, the din of their engines seemed louder than usual to her ears. She glanced after the man, but he had vanished, swallowed up in the crowds that were spewing out of Baker Street station or descending from buses. Swallowing hard, Natalia tried to rid herself of these disturbing thoughts, so frequent in recent months. The smallest thing could trigger a panic. She couldn't think about any of it now. It was too hard.

Moments later, it was almost a relief to walk through the automatic glass doors into the air-conditioned reception area of the Lost Property Office, and feel the ice-cold air flooding out. Five days a week, the general public came through those same doors in search of possessions, treasured or otherwise, mislaid or forgotten on London's vast transport system. They were greeted by a functional space, grey industrial carpeting underfoot, grey plastic chairs set against one wall, and a standard desk. For Natalia, it was the people she worked with that gave the place its colour and character.

In a short while, the reception area was going to be refurbished and updated, but for now it was its usual shabby and comfortable self. Natalia saw an elderly lady with fluffy, white hair sitting on one of the chairs, wearing an odd assortment of clothes, including a coat despite the hot weather outside. She smiled. It was Elsie, a rather vague lady who regularly visited them looking for things she'd mislaid. One day she'd come looking for her teapot, another for her spare petticoat. They listened to her, gave her a cup of tea, then sent her on her way. She was always good-humoured. Natalia guessed that coming to the LPO was a social outing for her. She waved to her, and Elsie waved cheerily back.

Wondering who would be manning the reception area today, Natalia worked out it was Wednesday, so that meant Avon, deputy manager, would be on duty. And that meant her annoying–

Toot toot!

And there it was, right on cue.

Passing through the chipboard dividers into the open-plan office beyond, Natalia was confronted by Avon brandishing an old-fashioned brass horn with a funnel one end, and a curling pipe and brown rubber bulb at the other.

'Not again, Avon,' Mark groaned, halfway across the office, bearing a cup of coffee from the machine.

Natalia shook her head, amazed at how

these English never swayed from their hot brews, no matter what the weather conditions were like outside. She was convinced that if global warming worsened to global boiling, they'd still be on the beaches in their protective suits, thermos in hand.

'Just testing. Got to be ready,' Avon insisted, squeezing the rubber bulb with relish. She'd been doing this for over a week now. Every time she connected a lost item with its rightful owner in fact – not counting all the other times, too. Constantly in motion, she was the type of employee who made everything look as if she were ten times busier, though in reality her workload was the same as everyone else's.

Mark met Natalia's clear-eyed gaze and rolled his eyes. She grinned back, while Avon bustled self-importantly around her desk, as ever.

'I'm on reception today,' Avon announced unnecessarily. 'So no slacking, you two.' And she gave another toot of her horn before placing it on her desk.

Still, there was something impressive about Avon, Natalia thought. The woman's spirit was indomitable. This week, her dramatically cut, sculptured bob was a rich chestnut. Natalia had given up guessing what her true

13

colour might be. A large woman, she knew how to dress herself to maximise her assets. Right now, she was wearing a crossover top in a green-and-white geometrical pattern over white trousers, which showed off the cleavage of her ample, size-sixteen figure. Smiling affectionately, Natalia had no doubt who she was trying to impress. But for now, there was no sign of Stefan.

'Sounds like her horn is badly in need of tuning,' Mark commented to Natalia, as he reached his desk, which was next to hers. Putting down his coffee, he plopped himself down into his swivel chair. 'Or does it just need putting out of its misery?' He made a strangling motion and winked.

'Mark, you wouldn't! Isn't there a direct-ive about cruelty to horns?'

'Health and Safety Rule 19, sub paragraph b. Horns only to be tooted once a day.'

'Or better, once a week.'

'Maybe there's a sanctuary for old horns?'

'That's a charity I'll support, little brother number two!'

Fifteen years her junior, Mark was still in his mid-twenties, and his mischievous air always reminded Natalia of her youngest brother back home in Krakow. Big, inno-cent blue eyes, dark hair cut in the latest

14

spiky style, short and sturdy. Football was Mark's big passion in life, just as it was her brother Jakub's. An East End lad born and bred though, Mark had told her he was a real 'barrer boy' and though she hadn't quite worked out what that meant, he certainly kept her entertained with his playful patter.

'Where did she find the thing anyway?'

They both looked at where the horn lay on Avon's desk, wondering how such a small thing could be so annoying.

'She logged it in last week. Couldn't bear to part with it, and she's been blowing her own trumpet ever since, da-dah!'

'Doesn't Donna have something to say?' Natalia asked, as she switched on her computer and put her handbag away in the bottom desk drawer.

'Donna's got her sights set on something higher,' Mark hinted.

'What now? I thought running the London Marathon in such good time would satisfy her goal setting for the time being.'

'Nah, that woman sets up more goals than midfielders at Stamford Bridge.'

Instinctively, they both glanced over at the glass windows of the partitioned-off office located at the side of the empty room, where their department boss, Donna, usually sat.

'She's after a special role as liaison officer between Lost Property working with British Transport Police, and the Metropolitan Police, no less.'

'Tch,' muttered Natalia. 'That woman – her middle name is "ambition". You get all the gossip, Mark.'

'Of course.' He tapped his nose. 'Remember, you heard it here first.'

'I'm going to get some water. Want some?'

'Thanks. I'd better drink some as well as my coffee. Otherwise I might overheat.'

Due to May's unprecedented heat wave, a water cooler had been installed beside Donna's office. Making her way across the room, greeting Ranjiv, Poppy and Jim as she passed them. A tight group who worked and lunched together, they were always polite to Natalia, but she'd yet to really befriend the old-timers. Like England, they were an island unto themselves.

Natalia stopped beside Rose, Donna's secretary's, desk, admiring the display of sweetly scented freesias and roses.

'What lovely flowers,' she said. 'Is it your birthday?'

Rose looked up shyly from the file she was studying. Her honey-brown hair, parted in the middle, fell in a classic bob to her jaw line. Her quiet demeanour meant that she was never flustered, whatever Donna and Avon got up to. Now, however, Natalia observed a faint tide of pink suffuse her face and neck, where a simple gold cross on a chain hung.

'Hello, Natalia. No, it's not my birthday. I don't know who they're from. They were here when I arrived.'

Not wanting to embarrass the girl with prying questions, Natalia excused herself and headed for the water cooler to fill two plastic cups. As she held the tab pressed down, she felt the breeze of Donna Harris passing her by. The department boss strode into her office, blonde hair sleek and still, a smart, black trouser suit and white shirt covering her trim form. She looked as cool as ever, unaffected by the heat.

So Donna was planning on liaising with the Met, Natalia mused. This wasn't a surprise. Donna was obsessed with the police. Donna and policemen, Natalia smiled to herself. It wasn't the uniform, and it wasn't only ambition, but Donna had a soft centre when it came to the power and authority of the police. Natalia knew her father had been a powerful army man in their homeland of

South Africa. Perhaps that had something to do with it.

Natalia carried the cups of water back, placing one on Mark's desk before sitting down at her own. As she did so, she glimpsed Cliff McDougal glancing out from the entrance to the vault. His small eyes under grey, beetling brows darted round the office. To a stranger, his demeanour would seem forbidding, indeed Natalia had found him frightening when she first met him, but she knew better now. She gave a quick nod, which he returned. She did not expect a smile, especially not this early in the day.

She drank some of the cool, clear water and that, coupled with the air conditioning, helped her begin to relax and let the early tensions slip away. Soon she would be lost in the familiar routine of assessing and logging in the myriads of objects, which were found and handed in at Underground and Overground stations, at bus depots and taxi offices all over the capital.

Toot TOOT!

Heads lifted, and there was a resounding sigh as Avon gave one final blast on her horn before heading at top speed for reception.

Thank goodness, Natalia thought, now for

18

some peace and quiet.

It was only when Cliff walked by her desk saying, 'Coming outside for a breath of air?' that Natalia realised it was three o'clock already.

'On your way to a ciggie break?'

'Aye.'

Natalia stood up to follow him, smelling the familiar aroma of tobacco smoke on his plaid shirt, which always brought back memories of her great-uncle Jan, who smoked a sweetbriar tobacco and pipe.

Even on such a hot day, Cliff's only concession was to leave off his trademark shapeless, brown jumper. She'd expected him to have quite a gut underneath, but he was relatively trim for his age, a well-worn, thick, leather belt holding up his corduroy trousers.

'You have to complete the *whole* form.' Natalia and Cliff were greeted by Avon's exasperated tones as they passed through the dividing partitions into the reception area. 'You've missed all this bit out.'

Avon stabbed at the paper on the desk so hard with one ring-clad finger that her immaculately polished nail left a red mark.

'I've put my name and address, and shown

19

you my latest electricity bill and passport. What more do you need?'

The young woman's voice was low, melodious, a tad uncertain. She put one hand up and pushed her thick, curly hair back behind her ear. Natalia saw that her nails were badly bitten and that her hair was left to tumble its way down wildly over her shoulders. She wore a floaty, full-length dress in dusty pink with tiny, primrose-yellow flowers. It had little puff sleeves from which her freckled arms poked out vulnerably, showing a scabbed graze on one elbow. She was a complete contrast to Avon's meticulous grooming.

Avon's brown eyes gleamed behind her glasses. She wanted to unite another lost item with its owner so that she could toot her horn. But this young woman was refusing to play the game.

'It says, quite clearly here "all boxes to be completed". Look.' Avon whisked the paper in front of the woman's eyes, making it impossible for her to read anything. 'You've got to tell us where you lost your necklace, or we can't take any further action.'

The young woman stared at the paper when Avon laid it down again. Her eyes filled with tears. 'I love that necklace. I've given you enough description, haven't I?'

Natalia lingered, although Cliff had already headed through the doors. Avon was taking her rules and regulations too far. The young woman was clearly sincere. She remained standing there, eyes downcast, the freckles on her face standing out in her milky skin.

'I told you, it's Art Deco Egyptian style. Gold settings with semi-precious stones. Peridot, carnelian, lapis lazuli and citrine.' She recited the names as if it were a poem learned long ago at her mother's knee.

'That's all very well, but I've got to know exactly when you lost it, and where. Where were you? On a train? Or a bus?'

The young woman shook her head. 'I ... I don't remember.'

Avon cast her eyes heavenward. 'I've keyed in the description on screen already and it's gone through to the vault, but I won't be able to release the necklace to you if you won't tell me more.'

The young woman looked up, biting her lip. 'I told you, I lost it two nights ago. I went out wearing it. When I looked the next day, it was gone. I haven't been burgled and I've searched my whole flat. So it must be out there somewhere,' she said, frustration clear

21

in her voice.

Natalia stepped closer, just as Stefan entered the reception area, carrying something.

'Is this what you want?' he said to Avon.

'Oh, thank you, Stefan.' Avon seemed to glow in Stefan's presence. Everyone in the office knew she had a crush on him. But she was one of many. With his black hair and dark, navy eyes Stefan had already broken many hearts. He grinned, winked at Natalia, and held out a gold necklace, with its LPO label tied neatly to it.

Natalia recognised it at once. She'd logged it in only yesterday.

'That's it!' the young woman gasped, her green eyes lighting up.

'You'll have to wait a moment, Stefan,' Avon commanded, clearly happy to keep him in reception with her. 'The forms haven't been completed yet.'

Natalia was aware that the customers queuing behind the woman were becoming restless, and beginning to mutter. One old chap said, 'Oh, give her the necklace, then we can all go home! Honestly, Job's-worth.'

'Just tell me where you lost the necklace and when – Friday you said? That's a start.'

The young woman hesitated. She was

about to speak when Avon continued, 'Now, a gold necklace, the fee for that'll be ten pounds, or should it be fifteen? What do you think, Stefan? It's in our discretion, but it does look expensive...'

Stefan looked at the necklace. 'Nice gold. Yes, I think twelve pounds, Avon. What happened?' He turned to face their customer. 'It has good clasp. How you lose it?'

The young woman gave an anguished, indignant gasp. 'Oh, keep it, why don't you?' she cried, turning and running out of the exit doors.

'About time. Now can we get some service?' the grumpy old man said.

'Oh, you two,' Natalia chided, snatching the necklace from Stefan's hand.

Her friend looked taken aback. 'What have I done?' he asked, but Natalia didn't stop to answer. She headed for the exit door.

'Wait, Natalia. Stop! That's Lost Property's property you've got. The forms haven't even been signed yet!' Avon called out.

Natalia ignored her, waiting for the exit doors to slide open enough for her to be able to pass through, eager not to lose sight of the young woman.

'Where the hell are you going?' Avon called again. But, as the doors started to close be-

23

hind her, the last thing Natalia heard was the sound of Avon's hooter.

Toooot!

2

A wall of heat greeted Natalia as the doors swished shut behind her. Immediately, perspiration began trickling down her back. Cliff was just pinching out the end of his cigarette.

'Sorry, Cliff, speak to you later,' Natalia called out.

He nodded. 'Aye, all right. I can see you're on a mission.'

He turned and went inside while Natalia desperately searched the street in both directions. She caught the flutter of a flowery, pink skirt, a tumble of hair, as the young woman stepped momentarily off the pavement to get round a circle of schoolchildren laughing and joking, upending bottles of water and spraying it at each other.

If she was heading for the tube, Natalia knew she had to hurry, before she was lost in the maze of tunnels and multiplicity of platforms at Baker Street station. Clutching the necklace safely tucked in her moist palm, she started down towards the Underground entrance, dodging to and fro around passers-by who were heading the other way, or strolling slowly in the same direction. She nearly tripped over two suitcases on wheels being pulled along by two smartly dressed businessmen, their jackets slung over their shoulders. And then she only just saved herself from knocking into a pregnant woman, as she saw the pink, floaty dress disappear into the marble entranceway of Baker Street station.

Fumbling in her bag for her Oyster card, Natalia pushed the necklace securely inside it, then closed the bag, holding it firmly under one arm. Not only because she would have to answer to Donna and Avon if she lost the necklace, or it was stolen – heaven forbid, it not having been signed for! – but, most importantly, because it clearly meant so much to the young woman she was chasing after.

Not stopping to take in her surroundings, the tempting arcades of Baker Street station, where she might normally linger and window shop, Natalia hurried through the ticket barriers and met a different kind of heat.

Stale air carried a mix of smells; food, hot human beings and the trains themselves.

Trapped at the top of an escalator by tourists, who were unused to the system whereby one was meant to stand on the right and leave the left of the stairs clear for those walking down them, Natalia at last had the young woman in her sights. She was glad she was wearing a flat pair of sandals, making her progress easier.

Natalia was at the bottom, pushing forwards, her sandals ringing out on the hard, stone flooring. The young woman turned under the arched gate topped by an old clock, heading for the Metropolitan and Circle Lines' platform. She seemed to know her way well, and hardly glanced up at the sign. She was not moving fast, apparently distracted, unaware of both her surroundings and the people passing by. Wasted on her were the posters advertising the West End's latest shows.

The young woman disappeared onto the platform, closely followed by Natalia. Walking to the farthest end, she sat down on a wooden bench. The platform was fairly empty, the overhead display indicating that a train for King's Cross and the City was due in five minutes.

As Natalia approached the young woman, she saw a middle-aged couple standing near her edge away. And then she could see why. The woman's eyes were red-rimmed and her face was streaked with tears. She was weeping quite openly, without making any attempt to wipe them away. A little bubble appeared at the end of her nose, then dropped onto her hands. Natalia sat down beside her.

'Hello,' she said.

The young woman looked at her without recognition.

'I'm Natalia O'Shea. I work at the Lost Property Office. I saw you just now.'

The young woman was distracted from her crying for a moment.

'Have you been following me? Why? What have I done now?' Her stare was resigned rather than defiant, her melodious voice hoarse from crying.

'Please, you've done nothing wrong. Nothing at all. I came to give you something.' Natalia opened her handbag, removed the necklace and held it out.

Immediately, the young woman's eyes widened in delight.

'My necklace!' she said, tentatively touching it, tears welling in her eyes again.

'Take it. It's yours,' Natalia proffered the necklace once more.

'Thank you. Thank you.' Natalia saw that her fingers were strong and calloused, as they closed on the jewellery, but her touch was delicate as she stroked the gold settings and then touched each gemstone in turn, calling out their names, almost singing them like an incantation: 'Peridot, carnelian, lapis lazuli, citrine...'

She looked at Natalia, smiling through her tears. 'This was my grandmother's. She passed it on to me when I turned sixteen. Alice, my dear gran. She led such a life when she was young. This was a gift from one of her admirers – a Russian count, she said.'

'She sounds quite a character,' Natalia said. 'Let me introduce myself again, Natalia O'Shea.'

'Polly Hansen.' The younger woman smiled through her rapidly drying tears. 'My grandmother would have liked you. She was very attractive, you know – red hair and green eyes. When she came over from Ireland, she had men flocking around her. That's where I get my freckles from,' she said ruefully, her eyes softening at the memories. 'She died ten years ago, age ninety.'

The overhead display now indicated that a Circle Line train was due in one minute, and a Metropolitan for Aldgate East in ten.

'My husband is from Dublin.' Natalia's voice was milky warm to reassure the distressed woman.

'My gran was from Cork. She practically raised me after Mum died. That's why the necklace means so much. It's such a personal item. So much history, you know.'

Natalia warmed to the young woman, her refined Irish accent was one of her favourites.

'It must be very hard,' she said, feeling her words were inadequate.

The hot air stirred and blew around them as a train approached. Polly made to stand up.

'Where was it found, my necklace, do you know?' she asked suddenly, fixing Natalia with her green eyes. 'I mean, do you get that kind of information? I just wondered, that's all.'

'We do always have that information, and I happen to know it well, because I was the person who logged in your necklace. I remember it clearly because I was thinking what a beautiful piece of jewellery it was, and very much hoped we would reunite it with its owner. I also remember thinking what a strange place it was for it to be found.'

'Where?' Polly looked anxious.

'Mornington Crescent station was where it was handed in. But it wasn't found on the platforms or in the lifts. That is what is so unusual.'

Polly became very still, listening intently.

The hot air stirred and blew around them as a train came roaring out of the tunnel and squealed to a stop.

'The night cleaners found it. One of them saw something gleaming on the floor. Your necklace. It had been partially jammed under a pipe. You're lucky it's not damaged. It was all in the docket notes.'

Natalia looked at Polly and saw she was looking down, frowning, fiddling with her dress.

'That's very strange,' she agreed. 'I wonder how it got there? The station isn't on my route home. I'd have headed for Camden Town.'

'I was wondering about that, too. It's not an area where the public have general access to.'

Polly shook her head slowly. 'I don't know. The thing is I ... I can't remember anything about last Friday night,' she said in a small voice.

The doors opened behind her and commuters shoved their way out onto the platform, while Polly and Natalia moved to the side.

'Why is that, Polly?'

Climbing onto the crowded carriage, Polly turned and held her hand against the door as she hurried to answer.

'Because ... because I was drunk.' An anguished look crossed Polly's face, as Natalia leaned in to catch her last hushed words. 'That's why. When I woke up, I was in the hallway just outside my flat. But I don't remember anything about getting home. The evening is just blank, blacked out. I don't know how my necklace got there. That's what scares me.'

And with that, the doors swished shut.

The last thing Natalia saw was the lonely figure of Polly squeezing her way past several people standing by the doors, disappearing into the crowd.

3

'Toot toot,' Mark sang out, as Natalia moved through reception and back to her desk, the atmosphere of jollity at odds with her mood.

'Toot toot,' chorused Stefan, standing at the entrance to the vault, calling out to her, too.

Natalia looked around and saw smiles on all her colleague's faces, including Rose's. There was no sign of Avon, though, or her horn.

'Toot toot?' she echoed questioningly. 'Where's Avon?'

'Gone home early,' Mark said cheerily. 'In high dudgeon.'

'In what?'

'In a huff,' Mark clarified.

'A huff and *a puff,*' Stefan called.

'Her hooter's gone walkabout and Avon is not best pleased. In fact, she looked fit to burst. She's accused us of all ganging up on her. A conspiracy to steal her hooter. And then she accused us each separately. Even you, despite the fact she was actually holding it when you left, Stefan told me. So she's gone home.'

'I think that's good news, isn't it? That her hooter's disappeared.'

Mark came over to stand by Natalia's desk. 'You'd think so. Nice and peaceful without it. Except Avon made up for it by stamping up and down blaming everyone except herself.'

'How did it disappear? Mark – it wasn't you up to one of your *pranks* was it?' Natalia was glad of the opportunity to use the word 'prank', which was new to her English vocabulary.

Mark adopted a very innocent expression. 'Me? Would I do something like that? I'm a choirboy, me.' And then he winked. Natalia laughed, glad for the distraction, still troubled by the lost look on Polly Hansen's face.

'You're my number-one suspect all the same,' she teased him in return. 'I shall grill you until you confess.'

Mark held up his hands. 'I'd give in now, if I'd done it. Your detective skills are second to none. I wouldn't stand a chance, with you on my tail,' he winked.

Natalia knew he was referring to the time before Christmas when she had helped

33

Peter Bookman find his missing wife, Helen. On that occasion, she had been drawn to Helen, connecting with her inner turmoil, which was so close to her own. But she continued to play the game. 'Come on now, Mark, tell me everything.' She stabbed her finger on her desk. 'Where were you when this terrible crime was committed? And where have you hidden the evidence?'

'The case of the 'orrible 'ooter!' Mark crowed. 'Or should it be the *curse* of the 'orrible 'ooter? No, it was like this. Avon went off to the ladies, only she left the offending article on the reception desk. When she came back, it was gone.'

'So it could be anyone. Even a member of the public.'

'Exactly. Maybe a kid snatched it. But Avon wouldn't have any of it. It had to be one of us.

'You know Avon won't forgive you for bucking the system. Those forms have to be filled in and signed. Course, she was already mad because you'd run off with that necklace. What happened there?' Mark tutted.

Natalia shrugged, not wanting to share something that was both painful and shameful to Polly with strangers. She'd had run-ins with Avon before. She seemed to see Natalia as a challenge and was always intent on stamping her authority on her. Every now and then they'd have a truce, but then Natalia would challenge the roles again. For her, people were more important than pieces of paper.

'I'll fill in the forms,' she told Mark. 'I know she lost the necklace at Mornington Crescent.'

'I'm sorry, Natalia, if I'd known she'd get so upset I wouldn't have pushed her.'

Stefan had quietly come to join them.

'It was a beautiful necklace.'

'It was her grandmother's,' Natalia told him, meeting her good friend's gaze, and silently acknowledging his apology.

'Aren't you going to interrogate Stefan about the missing you know what?' Mark asked.

'Very well. Stefan, where were you at approximately four o'clock, when the offending article was removed?'

Lounging against the desk, his arms crossed, his dark, navy eyes, fringed by long, black lashes, were as innocent as Mark's as he replied, 'I was in the vault, with Cliff, and thousands of lost objects.'

Natalia narrowed her eyes. 'Was that *all* the time?'

'All right, you have me – we went outside for a cigarette. But together. You will have to question Cliff, too.'

They all three looked towards the entrance of the vault and, as if he'd heard what they were saying, there was Cliff, glowering at them from beneath his bushy brows.

'Who's for the pub?' Mark said. 'It's nearly half-past five. Avon's gone home and Donna's still tied up in her meeting. She won't be back today,' he predicted. 'Coming, Stefan, Natalia?'

'A long, cold lager – I'm coming,' Stefan said. 'Natalia?'

She looked at her desk. After nine months at the LPO and with her English more fluent every day, she'd become adept at logging in, and her work was up to date. 'That'd be great. I have an hour, then I'm meeting Dermot at Camden Town. We're going to see a movie and then we're going to a Greek restaurant.'

As Natalia began to log off, Cliff called out, 'Are you lot skiving again? Where's Avon?'

'Gone home,' Mark told him. 'Can't get over the loss of her hooter.' He lifted an imaginary horn to his lips and gave a long soft 'tooooot'.

'We're going to the pub,' Natalia offered.

'Aye, are you no coming for a wee dram?' Mark said.

Cliff ignored the mangling of his Scottish accent. 'Someone's got to look after the place,' he growled, and disappeared back inside the vault.

Mark and Stefan looked at one another, grinning, and winked.

'What?' Natalia demanded.

'Nothing,' they both said in unison, then burst out laughing.

'You know something about Cliff?' she pressed them.

'Well–' Mark looked at Stefan.

'We know *some*thing, but–' Stefan said.

'About what he gets up to when no one's around.'

'He thinks no one knows. But I see him one day.'

'Tell me,' Natalia begged.

'Uh uh,' Mark denied her.

'Maybe one day,' Stefan said. 'But now I am longing for that beer.'

Natalia idly wondered what Cliff could be up to that he didn't want anyone to know about. Had he taken up embroidery? Or was he practising ballroom-dancing steps? She pictured him practising staccato fox-trot steps down the aisles between the shelving.

She followed Mark and Stefan, and glanced over at Rose, wondering if she would like to join them. But, as if sensing what she was about to ask, Rose bent over her task, studiously avoiding meeting Natalia's gaze. So Natalia contented herself with calling out, 'Night, Rose,' and took one last look at the beautiful flowers on her desk.

Outside, the drifting aromas of frying onions and chips from restaurant air vents mingled with the acrid smell of petrol fumes. Immediately, Natalia felt perspiration prickle on her skin again. Her linen trousers were well creased now. The unexpected May heatwave that had lingered on into June had brought out the golden highlights in her fine, pale-brown hair, which fell to below her shoulders, and fetched admiring glances from men passing by.

Stefan's lean and lanky frame seemed unaffected by the heat. His jeans fitted loosely over his narrow hips, his pale-blue shirt, worn outside his jeans, seemed as fresh as it had when he'd arrived that morning. He drew lustful looks from women of all ages.

For once, though, Stefan was not responding. Perhaps he had not recovered yet from the shock of turning thirty, and the big party he'd held to celebrate it. Natalia's own older brother, Karl, who had also cut a swathe through the female population, had suddenly decided to settle down when he was thirty. But she'd not seen any slowing down yet of Stefan's conquests.

Mark was the shortest of the three, his open shirt revealing a wisp of chest hair. His life was devoted to sport, watching it, that is. He had nearly landed himself in trouble at work with his obsession for fantasy football last year, and was on the brink of getting hooked on the gambling side, but general concern from friends had pulled him back. When is a girl going to distract him from the Beautiful Game, Natalia wondered. Only if she's wearing his favourite team's strip, Stefan had told her once. She berated herself for not remembering whether that was Tottenham Hotspur or not.

The Case Solved was only a few minutes walk, and thankfully air-conditioned. Unsurprisingly, the modern decor was Sherlock Holmes themed, whose fictional address of 221B Baker Street was only a few doors from the LPO itself

'What're you having?' Mark said. 'My round. Natalia?'

'White wine spritzer, please, with lots of ice.'

'I'll have a San Miguel,' Stefan said, then, 'Let's find somewhere to sit.'

They found a table near the entrance, where the glass doors had been folded back and tables spilled outside, but where it was still cool.

'How's Dermot?' Stefan asked, but as Natalia opened her mouth to reply, his phone beeped and he glanced at it. 'Sorry, I'll just answer this,' he said. She watched his mouth curve into a smile as his thumbs flew over the phone, answering the text message. It would be one of his girlfriends, but there was no point in asking her name or anything about her. She'd be gone by next week, replaced by another.

Natalia relaxed back into her chair. The London pub was one institution she had adapted to with great ease. At first she'd felt nervous entering by herself, especially if the person she was meeting – usually Dermot – wasn't there yet. But she soon found that a woman could order a drink and sit by herself, reading the paper, without attracting unwanted attention or being made to feel unwelcome. Occasionally, a man might meet her eye, but if she didn't respond, he wouldn't hassle her. She'd had some interesting conversations with strangers in bars, too, who usually wanted to learn more about Poland. It seemed that women in England could happily go to clubs and pubs just to have a good time together, if that's all they wanted.

Had Polly, on her night out last Friday, just wanted a good time? Was she a regular binge drinker or was it an unusual occurrence for her to get so drunk that she suffered memory loss?

Mark's arrival with the drinks interrupted Natalia's thoughts. 'Look who's here,' he said.

'Hi, guys,' a young, good-looking Jamaican man approached. It was Jason, Natalia's friend Rasheda's son.

Ever since he'd passed the exams for the British Transport Police and had started working in the BTP's London Underground division, Natalia and the team had been seeing a lot more of him, and all had grown quite friendly. Jason's black eyes always sparkled with good humour. Out of his BTP uniform, his tight shirt showed off his impressive physique. 'I'll get my own drink and join you – I'm waiting for Honey.' That was his girlfriend, whom Natalia had met on a number of occasions recently. Honey was as gorgeous as a model, but shy and quiet. Stefan, clearly remembering the last time *he* saw Honey, immediately looked interested.

'Cheers!' Mark, Stefan and Natalia clinked glasses. 'Am I glad to get away from Avon and her horn,' Mark observed. 'She was really getting up my hooter today. Boom boom! So, Jase, how's the new job going?'

'Fan bloody tastic.' Jason took a swig of his half pint of beer. 'I'm doing weekends, see. Get all the action on Fridays and Saturdays.'

'Explains why you're not in uniform.'

'S'right. Me day off. Oh but, man, this town is buzzing at the weekend. You wouldn't believe some of the stuff that goes down.'

'Are you still based in North London?' Natalia asked. She could see that Jason had just the right temperament to deal with members of the public, particularly if they'd been caught out in a misdemeanour. Upbeat, cheery, able to exchange backchat in a firm but non-threatening way.

'Yeah,' he said. 'Kentish Town, Camden, up to Holloway and Archway. As far as the Crouch End border.'

'Busy neighbourhood,' Mark said.

'Just listen to this. The other night, there

was this feller, right, he's coming up the tunnel, like this.' He did an imitation swagger. 'Wearing a baseball cap and shades – how uncool is that? – down the Underground. Sees me and Jack standing there in our uniforms, like, and he's gone. Makes a run for it. Charges right at us. I was going to take him, but Jack shoves me, see.' He demonstrated again. 'So the guy goes between us but Jack sticks his foot out, the guy stumbles and we get him from behind. He was carrying a knife. I didn't see it, but Jack did. One more knife off the streets. And he'd only travelled one stop without a ticket. What an idiot.'

He shook his head and ran his hand over his short, cropped hair. He had high cheekbones, black eyes and caramel-coloured skin, and looked more like the one snapshot Natalia had seen of his father, than his mother Rasheda. While Stefan was physically fit, Jason's well-toned musculature was shown off by his tight-fitting brown top.

'Jack,' Natalia said. 'Is that Detective Sergeant Jack Riley?'

'That's right. You know him? He's amazing. He's quite senior to me, but sometimes I get teamed up with him or I can just go to him and ask questions. He's seen it all, knows all the angles. I'm learning a lot from him.'

'He's liaison officer with us,' Natalia told him. 'He took over from some man called Jonathan Crane after Christmas, when he got fast-tracked.'

A sudden cheer caught Mark's attention. 'I don't believe it,' he said to Stefan. 'The Croatians have scored again.'

While Stefan and Mark were looking at the football, Natalia asked Jason, 'How's your mum? I don't see so much of her these days. She's not doing so many night shifts.' Previously, Rasheda had worked as much overtime as possible to fund her younger son Daniel through coaching for his GCSEs. 'I expect your wages come in handy now.'

'She's had something on her mind lately.' Jason grew serious. 'It's my dad. He's due out next week.' Suddenly his grin was back. 'I'll have to hang on to my wallet. The old man can charm the birds out of the trees, when he's a mind to.'

'He's coming out of prison early then?' Natalia asked, surprised. Rasheda had not said anything to her, but suddenly her friend's subdued behaviour of recent weeks made everything fall into place. No wonder her friend had been so withdrawn. Ray-

44

mond, the father of her two boys – they'd never officially married – spent periodic spells at Her Majesty's Pleasure for his wheeling and dealing on the street, primarily ganja that he sourced from family back in Jamaica. This meant that Jason had had to go through more-stringent security checks than some, to join the police service.

What would she decide to do? Natalia wondered. There was no rulebook when it came to matters of the heart. Jason had once confided to her that he thought his mother still carried a torch for his dad. The impression Natalia had was of a loveable rogue, whose illegal activities hurt no one but himself, although the debate as to whether weed was a useful medicinal and recreational drug, or something that led to harder drugs, still raged. And what about the odd dodgy, second-hand motor? If not checked properly, they could also kill.

Rasheda would not only be asking herself these questions, she'd be thinking about Raymond's influence on their younger son. She would want Daniel to have a male role model, but the boy was more sensitive and suggestible than his older brother. He hadn't made up his mind about where his allegiances lay. Rasheda would not find an

45

easy answer.

'Good behaviour, innit. I told you, he can charm anyone.' Jason glanced at his watch. 'Time to get another round in before Honey arrives, and I'll get a glass of wine for her. We're going to a rock concert tonight. Same again?' Mark and Stefan came over and put their orders in while Natalia shook her head.

'I'll come with you and help carry them,' Mark said.

'My round next time,' Stefan said.

As Jason and Mark reached the bar, Honey walked in. Black hair bouncing over her shoulders, she wore a strapless summer dress in black with large, white dots, held up with a red cummerbund under her breasts. She gave her shy smile and Jason put an arm round her and they kissed. Natalia heard Stefan sigh.

'What's the matter, my brother?' she asked.

'Jason's a lucky guy, I'm thinking.'

'You haven't fallen for Honey, have you?' Natalia felt a stab of concern. That might explain his occasional moodiness recently.

'No. She's a lovely girl, but she's his girl. I don't steal from friends.' Natalia suppressed a smile at Stefan's unspoken confidence that

46

he could have any girl he chose. He was most likely ninety-nine per cent right. 'Jason's lucky because he knows what he wants, and he's got it. They have a future together.'

'What, not thinking of hanging up your pulling pants?' Mark teased, overhearing Stefan's comment as he returned with their drinks. 'Or have you been turned down for once?'

Stefan flushed slightly. 'Not me, mate. I am never turned down. Give me five minutes and I'll have that redhead's number.'

He walked over to a tall, leggy redhead at the bar.

'Mark, you should be ashamed. Another girl's heart will be broken.'

Mark shrugged. 'I don't know why they can't see right through him. I do. So what are you and Dermot going to see tonight?'

'It's a film from the Czech Republic. Very good.'

'The sort that would send me to sleep then! Give me a superhero any time.'

Natalia finished her drink and stood up. 'I must go now, or I'll be late.' She waved goodbye to Honey and Jason.

Stefan approached, waving a piece of paper. 'See?' he said to Mark. 'My pulling

47

trousers are still working.' As Mark groaned and rolled his eyes, Natalia waved goodbye, taking her leave of them.

4

'The whole world is out on the street tonight,' Natalia declared, her arm tucked into Dermot's. She still loved it when he stuck his elbow out, hand in pocket, a true gentleman, for her to put her hand through.

They were strolling slowly towards Camden Town tube station shortly after ten o'clock on this hot, early June night. Knots of people from every corner of the globe filled the pavements, talking, laughing, sitting at tables outside cafes, restaurants and pubs. From one direction, she could hear the sound of a steel band, from another a fusion band. It was a cacophony, a mixing bowl of cultures, Natalia thought, like turning the tuner on a radio and running through hundreds of different stations.

'It's always lively up here in Camden, so it is, but tonight it's the heat as well.'

'I can't believe you've never eaten Greek

before,' Dermot said. 'Not even been to the Greek islands. We'll have to do something about that.' He squeezed her arm with his. 'Or maybe the Croatian islands. How about going away for a few days for our wedding anniversary?'

Their eyes met and Natalia felt the familiar desire for her husband surge in her, as warm as when they'd first been together.

'We haven't had a chance for many holidays together yet, have we?' he continued softly. 'This'll be our second anniversary, and we didn't have a proper honeymoon first time round.' They'd been saving towards buying their own place, and had just visited Natalia's relatives in the country. 'I wonder what a second anniversary is called? Stone or mud or something, I expect.'

'Huh. What about ribbons or daisies?'

'Very girly, Nat,' he said, still in that soft tone he reserved for their most intimate moments. 'I say we start planning for early September.'

'What about the children?'

He lifted an eyebrow. 'You want them to come on our second honeymoon? Love them as I do, I don't think even *I* would want them there.'

She thought of Nuala, Dermot's daughter,

and Connor, his son. Nuala was so like her father, with his dark-blue eyes, but she spent hours in front of the mirror straightening the black, curly hair she'd inherited from him. Thirteen now, she was fully absorbed in her passion for learning to sing and perform on stage. Connor at nine looked more like his mother Kathleen, with silvery, fair hair and china-blue eyes. As long as he could play football and computer games with his dad, his universe was complete.

'They seem to be getting along fine now. Do we want to upset things, just as they're beginning to get used to me?'

'And to having me in their lives, too,' Dermot said, referring to the years when his ex-wife Kathleen had moved their children from Dublin to London, cold to the fact that he was tied to Ireland by a big construction contract. Furious and hurt, virtually all contact had been severed by the time his next contract brought him to Poland, where he'd lodged with Natalia's family. Gradually, she and her family had brought him back to life again. 'Tell you what, darlin', we'll talk to them and arrange lots of family outings during school holidays to compensate. How's that?'

'Very good idea. And then I can get to see

some of these famous places, too, theme parks, Tower of London.'

'Buckingham Palace? No, I can picture Nuala's face. Plenty of shops for her.'

'Maybe the Theatre Museum, or the BBC to see a show being recorded. She might find that interesting.'

'Good idea. Natural History Museum'll be perfect for Connor, though. He still loves dinosaurs.'

As they strolled slowly along, they paused to check out different restaurant menus for another night, idly gazing in the windows of the eclectic mix of shops. Coming to a halt, Dermot paused outside the window of a Turkish restaurant.

Natalia watched a couple exit, holding the door open for friends. Then her gaze returned to the door, as she saw inside the restaurant. Something had caught her attention, and her breath nearly stopped. Jem. Could it be him? She stared at the back of a tall, slim man with wide shoulders. He wore blue jeans and a white shirt with short sleeves. His hair was thick and jet black. He was holding onto the shoulder of a boy, about ten years old. Also with his back to her.

As the couple's friends exited, and the

51

door was about to shut, the man turned round.

It wasn't Jem. And so it wasn't Paul, her son. Their son.

Natalia let her breath go, but the tearing longing inside her stayed. Once again, her hopes had been raised, only to be dashed. She'd last seen Paul in the flesh when he was four years old. Snatched from his kindergarten by Jem, and smuggled out of Poland to Turkey, where Jem's family had at first closed ranks around him, no amount of searching had revealed the whereabouts of her little boy.

Natalia didn't know how she got through the next few years. The support of her family and friends helped her to cope. And then Dermot had come into her life. She'd been lucky enough to find love the second time around. The thought of Dermot still brought a smile to her face. But now she was faced with a dilemma that challenged her marriage. She was going to have to make a decision. And whichever route she chose, heartache would follow.

Involuntarily, Natalia tensed. Dermot felt her do so.

'Sorry, darlin', I didn't think.' He made to walk on, but she stopped him.

'No, it's all right. I'm just being silly. I love Turkish food. It's wonderful – look at this fantastic starter plate.' She tried to concentrate but the words were blurring in front of her.

'You'll find him again,' Dermot said, quietly reassuring. 'I know you – we – will find your Paul.'

Paul. She closed her eyes for a second and the image of her ten-year-old son from the most recent photograph, received at Christmas, floated in front of her again.

'If I hadn't seen the return address Fatima wrote on the back of the envelope and written back to her, well,' Natalia shivered, despite the heat, 'I'd never have found out Jem had brought Paul to live in the UK. But where?'

'My guess is that's the only reason your sister-in-law felt she wasn't being disloyal to him, putting down her address for the first time, because your ex had left Turkey for England.'

'But why has he come here?' Natalia asked the question that no one had been able to answer yet.

Stopping at traffic lights, they waited to cross to the station entrance. Traffic flowed on all sides of them, passing up towards

Kentish Town, Holloway and north London, or southbound to King's Cross.

'I would settle for any clue right now.' Natalia said, as the lights changed and the green man was illuminated, accompanied by a beeping sound, telling them it was safe to cross. 'Just to see Paul, to hold him again. Now and then. To know that he knows I still love him.' Her throat closed with all-too-familiar grief.

Natalia's steps dragged on the molten pavement. In her mind's eye she replayed pictures of Paul, as a baby, as a toddler, that last moment when he'd waved to her as he ran into his kindergarten. And, more recently, the annual photo sent secretly by her sister-in-law.

Dermot had hold of her hand now and she felt his grip tighten. They'd talked about it so many times since Christmas. He'd not complained once about the long hours she spent on the Internet, the letters she wrote, the phone calls she made, all in the fruitless search for a sign, a hint, a clue as to where Jem and Paul might be. All of it bringing back again the terrible pain and deep despair she'd felt in the wake of Paul being taken away from her.

And although it was exciting to know that

Paul was now that much closer to her, it also brought Jem closer, too, and the memory of those months of threats of physical violence. She found herself seeing Jem everywhere, fearing his hand on her shoulder, hearing his angry voice yelling.

'Yes, we must stay positive. All the searching will bring a result,' she said. 'I won't give up.'

Reaching the ticket hall, they used their Oyster cards to pass through the ticket barriers.

'What's going on here?' Dermot halted, and Natalia bumped into him.

In the middle of the pedestrian hallway, spread across and preventing access to the lifts and stairs to the people coming in from the front and side entrances of the station, were two men and two women in official uniforms. British Transport Police. One of the men held the leash of an alert, healthy-looking dog: a brown-and-white spaniel, its tail wagging as it stood obediently beside its handler.

Then Natalia saw a fifth official, wearing a black uniform and peaked cap that bore the word Inspector. But he wasn't your typical ticket inspector, not with an armed guard.

'What's the dog doing here?' Natalia asked

Dermot, as they were held up in the queue of people.

'It's a sniffer dog. Looking for drugs. If it was an Alsatian dog, I guess they'd be expecting to have to chase someone.'

Those travellers in front of them wanting to go down and catch a train pressed forward, as each had their ticket or Oyster card inspected. Those coming up also had to show they'd paid their fare. The rumble of a train beneath their feet announced the arrival of more passengers.

Natalia noticed the dog handler only allowed his dog to approach certain individuals.

'Looks like they've had some sort of tip off,' Dermot said. 'Some drugs coming through this station.'

An altercation started between a young woman pushing a pushchair with a toddler in it, and with another small child at her side, and one of the officers.

'No good giving me a fine,' she shouted. 'I've no money, me. Why'd you think I ain't got no ticket you effing–'

'OK, OK, calm down.' The young policewoman was hiding a smile at the young mother's colourful, blustering language. 'Give me your address, love, and we won't press any charges, but you'll have to leave the station. They might not be so gentle with you at the other end.'

With another burst of colourful language about being forced to leave before she'd been able to get on a train, the young woman complied and gave her address.

'How did she get in without a ticket?' Natalia wondered.

'Used the children as distraction probably, getting through the luggage gate.'

But Natalia's attention had been caught by something else.

'Look over there.' She nudged Dermot with her elbow. 'That's the third person they've set the sniffer dog on, and they all looked the same. Bulgarian or Romanian, I think.'

'I noticed,' Dermot agreed. 'All three look Eastern European.'

Natalia held back, watching as the man started fumbling in his pockets while the dog continued to sniff around his old combat trousers, wrinkled at the ankles over badly scuffed trainers. The dog looked up eagerly now, and then at his handler. The two Transport Police, one male, one female, stood either side of him. Not deliberately intimidating, but standing firm nonetheless.

57

The man was shorter than them. His skin was swarthy and badly scarred with acne, and dark stubble etched the outline of his jaw. His black hair stood up in tufts and his eyes darted nervously from side to side as he tried to appease the police.

'Please,' he was saying. 'Papers at house. No illegal.'

'I need to see your ticket,' the policewoman said, enunciating carefully. 'Your tick-et.'

'Ticket at house. Good man. Good work.' He struck his chest and spoke again in his own language. It was not Polish, but Natalia thought she recognised some words.

The policeman produced his handheld PC and said, 'What's your address? Where is your house?'

The Eastern European man became more animated. He shook his head. 'Please, I good work. No problems.'

'All right, sir, no one's saying you don't have work,' the policewoman said. 'But we have to check where you live. Is your home in Camden Town?'

The man spoke again in his native tongue, seeming to shrink down into his jacket, which was frayed and worn at the collar and cuffs. Natalia began to start forward. Surely there was something she could do to help.

Maybe he understood Polish, or a little Russian.

'No, Natalia. Stay out of it. Come on, we'd best get home.' Dermot's arm restrained her. He ushered his wife forward through the ticket inspection, and they went on their way to the platform.

'I know,' Dermot said. 'You think I'm a hard man. But I think the police were doing a good job there. They weren't abusing the guy, or hitting on him at all.'

'He seemed so lost and bewildered. He didn't understand the word ticket, perhaps. Anyway, is that such a crime, not paying your fare?'

'Well, if too many people went without paying, the tube would be in a worse state than it is now. And some of these guys are con artists. I know, I've employed a few in my time.'

'But there are worse crimes going on all around us. People suffering violence, living in fear. Much worse than fare dodging.'

'Only it wasn't just fare dodging, was it? That sniffer dog shows they were after some-thing more serious. Drugs – maybe chemicals of some kind. Bomb-making equipment. Had you thought of that?'

'Searching for drugs and bombs. That's

59

always the excuse for the police interfering in our lives.'

'Think about it, darlin'. The odd puff of marijuana may be nothing, but heroin, crack, meth – that's a world where everyone loses and gets hurt, not just the user. They'll do anything, go to any lengths to get their next fix and it doesn't matter who gets injured or worse along the way.'

Natalia shifted uncomfortably. Hadn't she had the same argument with herself, about Rasheda's partner, whose activities had landed him in prison on many occasions?

'Maybe he was an illegal immigrant? And if so, why shouldn't they pick him up? He could be part of the trade in smuggling human beings about Europe, which makes a few villains rich, and treats these people like slaves. Or he could've made his own way here and be receiving benefits when he hasn't paid anything into the system himself. Is that fair, when our budgets are stretched to the limit already? I don't know about the rights and wrongs, but I know there's no easy answer.'

'OK, OK, you can get off your soapbox. Immigrants are a problem in this country for one reason or another–'

Natalia broke off and stared at Dermot

and he stared back then, as they felt the rush of warm air heralding the arrival of their train, they both laughed. 'Look at us, immigrants both!'

'But strictly legal,' he added.

The train halted and the doors slid open. They climbed in and found two seats side by side. The late-evening train was so different from the quiet of commuter time. Young people laughed and called to each other, sitting on each other's knees, using a babel of different languages.

Dermot smiled at Natalia. 'How about it, love?' he said. 'How about adding another immigrant of our own to this land?' Impulsively, he laid a hand on her stomach.

Natalia felt the familiar ache as her heart was pulled in two directions. She laid her hand on top of his, not wanting to look up into his eyes and see the shadow that would cross them as he heard her words.

'You're such a good father,' she told him. 'You must believe that.' How she wanted to grant him his wish. A baby of their own. She could see him now, tenderly cradling the baby, playing with the toddler on his knee – but then, every time, the toddler would have Paul's face and it would be Jem tossing him in the air, Jem cuddling him tight. She couldn't betray Paul's memory when she still did not know where he was. She needed to make sure for herself that he was all right.

Beside her, Dermot stiffened and pulled away. 'I know. I'm sorry I brought it up again,' he said resignedly. 'I do understand, Natalia.'

Each time they had this conversation, her heart frayed a little more as she feared the strain she was putting on their relationship. She loved Dermot with all her being and couldn't bear to hurt him, to push him away. But what of Paul? He was just a little boy.

5

Origin of find: Mornington Crescent. Natalia's fingers flew over the keyboard as she continued to log in the details of her next item. Each lost object that was found on the London Transport system, whether by a member of the public or a member of staff, carried with it full details of where and when it was found and where it was handed in. Donna had recently informed them that in the previous year 130,000 objects were handed in. This year it was sure to be even higher.

Sometimes, a lost object carried details about the owner. If not an actual address or phone number, then other clues. Each member of the LPO staff was tasked with following these up and contacting the owner directly, if possible. Only a third of all the lost items handed in were claimed, however. Natalia could understand why Donna wanted to give the LPO a higher profile, so that more people would come to them for their possessions.

For now, she was keeping their computer system, appropriately called 'Sherlock', very busy. Each item was firstly assigned a reference number. Then came one of Natalia's favourite moments. Writing the number on an old-fashioned brown label and tying it to the object with the strings.

When she and her office colleagues had done their job, the item was then handed into the care of Cliff, who, in turn, allocated it its space on the miles of shelving in the vault. This was Cliff's kingdom, which he ruled over with the help of Stefan.

Mornington Crescent. She slowed down

and looked at what she'd entered into Sherlock. It was a distinctive make-up bag. The tag on the zip indicated that it came from Harvey Nichols, the smart Knightsbridge store. It was a shiny, bronze colour. Inside, was a palette of eye shadow and cheek and lip colour by Bobbi Brown, all in plum and purple shades. And a Touche Eclat wand by Yves St Laurent. She had noticed that the cover of the palette was cracked and a corner had fallen off, and the Touche Eclat wand was bent.

Mornington Crescent. That was where Polly's necklace had been found last week. She leaned back in her chair and stretched her arms and legs and wiggled her toes, taking a moment away from the computer screen. Mark's dark head was bent over his keyboard, Ranjiv was gazing into the distance and Tom seemed to have fallen asleep. Even Avon's flame-coloured hair – she'd added blonde streaks this week – seemed subdued as the heat from outside fought their air-conditioning, inducing a lethargic atmosphere. There was nothing lethargic about Avon's temper this morning though. She was still convinced that one of her co-workers had taken her horn, and had already rounded on Rose about it. Although Rose would surely be the least likely possible suspect.

Mornington Crescent. Funny coincidence that. But then again, why not? It was a reasonably busy station and perfectly possible that objects should have been lost there two weeks in a row. Natalia tried to be rational, telling herself just to do her job and to move on to the next item. Yet the feeling that Polly's necklace and this makeup bag were somehow connected wouldn't let her go. She scrolled back and read through the details again. The make-up bag had been found at the bottom of the steps that led to the platforms, but not the normal stairs. No, just inside the fire door that lay in one of the cross routes from southbound to northbound platforms. It was certainly strange, but quite possible that it had been moved along there during security checks on the doors, or during cleaning.

Frowning, Natalia tapped at the keyboard and brought up the closed file about Polly's necklace. Of course. Her necklace had also been found in a restricted area, beyond the fire door. And on the same day of the week. A Tuesday. Polly had lost her necklace on a Friday night. It took, on average, at least two days for lost objects to find their way to the

LPO – at worst, as much as two weeks. So, finding it on a Tuesday, could that be significant? She brought up the make-up bag details, then looked back at Polly's. In both instances they'd been found by a member of the cleaning staff. That was it. He or she must clean that area weekly.

She mulled over how unusual it could be, to have two items belonging to women, lost in a restricted area at the same Underground station. She remembered how distressed Polly had been, and also how she could not remember where she had been that night. Could she have found her way in there somehow?

Still frowning in concentration, Natalia tapped in instructions for a crosscheck on Camden Town/Mornington Crescent stations since the beginning of the year. She didn't expect to find anything. But what she did see brought a rush of alarm. Many objects had been handed in at Camden Town, of all types. The usual books, clothes, umbrellas, a skateboard and, most bizarrely, a set of bowling balls. But none of them had been found anywhere unusual.

Mornington Crescent was a less busy station. Fewer items had been handed in. But, starting back in May, Natalia could see that items had been trickling through. Items distinctively belonging to women, which had been found outside the areas normally used by passengers. No member of staff had laid claim to them. Besides Polly's necklace, there was a brooch in the shape of a cat, a lipstick, and an ankle bracelet with a small charm of a yin and yang symbol on it. The pin on the brooch had been bent. Polly was the only woman who had come to claim any of these lost objects. Natalia was sure she had only come because the necklace meant so much to her, being handed down from her gran.

Clearly seeing a pattern here, Natalia instructed the computer to print off a copy of each file. Then she read them through again to double check, all the time thinking, Polly could not recall anything about her night out. What was happening to these women? She looked up. Yes, Donna was in her office. She had to show the department boss what she'd discovered. She had to pass this information on to the police.

She crossed to Donna's office. Inside, she could see that her shiny, blonde hair was clipped up at the back of her head in a business-like fashion, the collar of her crisp, white shirt turned down over the black gilet she wore, even on such a hot day. Rose sat at her desk outside. A single red rose stood in a vase beside her computer.

'I'd like to have a word with Donna,' Natalia requested.

Rose nodded. 'As long as you make it quick. The Area Commander of the BTP is due in to see her shortly.'

Natalia nodded and knocked on Donna's door. She knew what that was about, thanks to Mark and the office grapevine.

'Natalia. How are you?' Donna gave her a quick smile, eyes never straying too far from the papers on her desk.

'I've noticed something unusual in the lost objects. A pattern,' Natalia told her.

'I see.'

'It's at Mornington Crescent. Look, these files show that on what seems to be the same night of the week, a Friday or maybe a Saturday, women are losing personal items – but not in the usual passageways. In restricted areas.'

'What?' Donna looked startled. 'You mean there's been trespassing going on? Hardly our remit.'

'No, not that. These objects are sometimes damaged. Who is taking these women to this secluded spot? And are they going willingly?' There, she'd voiced it. The concern that had been growing in her mind.

Donna snorted. 'That's a big leap from a handful of lost objects that, may I remind you, we receive thousands of all the time, to women being attacked on the Underground.'

'Only one woman has been in to claim her lost jewellery. Polly Hansen. And this is the thing. She cannot remember anything about her Friday night. Where she was ... what she did.'

Donna snorted again. 'She's hardly alone in that, is she?'

'But what happened to her? Please look at these files. I think we should notify the police. Rose mentioned an Area Commander is coming in–'

'Oh, I don't think we want to bother him with a small matter like this. I'm sure it's just a coincidence. If we started looking for patterns in the lost objects brought in, we'd be seeing them everywhere. And they would all be meaningless.'

Natalia knew she had to stand her ground with Donna. That's what her boss understood. 'I have worked here nine months now. I don't see anything like this before. Look here, and here – and here. Always the same time of week. Always a restricted area.'

'Hmm.' Donna stood up. 'I have a meeting now. But keep an eye on it. Monitor the situation. Let me know if it happens again, all right?'

She handed Natalia's papers back to her and started to inexorably usher her towards the door.

But Natalia was insistent. 'I am worried about this young woman, Polly. Why could she not remember what happened to her? She did not need to use Mornington Crescent station to get home.'

'So she met someone. It's not against the law, you know. As I said,' Donna repeated firmly as they came out of her office and stood beside Rose's desk, 'monitor the situation and report back to me.'

Aware that Avon was watching their every move, Natalia persisted, aware she was pushing Donna's patience to the limit. But she could not forget Polly's pain and bewilderment. That took precedence. 'Your meeting now is with the British Transport Police Area Commander?'

'That's right, Jonathan Crane,' Donna answered reluctantly.

'Why not show him the papers? Let him decide if he sees something he can take

70

action on. It would only take five minutes of his time.'

'Jonathan is a powerful and busy man.' Natalia saw a faint blush stain Donna's neck. And she was wearing a short skirt today, to display her shapely calves and ankles. So she still had a crush on Jonathan Crane, the Area Commander. 'I doubt he'll have time for this.'

'Just two minutes then of his time,' Natalia persisted. Avon was still eavesdropping, looking past Cliff, who was standing at her desk beside Rose's.

'If it's a policeman ye're after, there's one in reception. I saw him just now when I was coming in from my ciggy break.'

'Thank you, Cliff.' Donna turned as if to go back in her office, changed her mind, looked at Rose, opened her mouth, then changed her mind again and set off towards reception. She's got it really bad again, Natalia thought. Donna was normally cool, calm and collected, but when she lusted after someone her defences were well and truly down.

Natalia followed Donna, passing through the dividers into reception. But what was Donna doing? She had stopped beside the reception desk, but had not greeted her visi-

71

tor. Instead, she nodded stiffly and turned to help Ranjiv, who was manning reception at that moment. Natalia moved forward, and immediately found her answer. Standing to one side, near the entrance doors, was a policeman – but not Jonathan Crane. She recognised him and understood Donna's reaction. It was Detective Sergeant Jack Riley, Jason's partner and Jonathan Crane's replacement. Donna had had a major crush on Jonathan Crane for months before he was transferred. And even though Jack was a good-looking, decent guy, he was no Jonathan Crane, apparently. Donna had been decidedly cool towards him, since he started.

'I'll take this one,' Donna was saying to Ranjiv. 'It's nearly home time now, you may as well go.'

'Thanks, Donna,' Ranjiv said, giving Natalia a puzzled look as he passed back into the office.

A movement from outside caught her eye. Could this be the Area Commander coming now? Was that why Jack was here? Had he been ordered to attend the meeting? That would make things awkward for Donna. But no, happily she saw the familiar outline of her friend Rasheda outside, reporting early for the nightly clean of the LPO offices. They'd only talked very briefly in the past few week. Rasheda had still not mentioned that Raymond was coming out of prison soon, and what she was going to do about it.

Jack walked towards the reception desk, and formed a queue behind a woman wearing a sari. As Natalia remembered, his expression was friendly and open. His brown hair was cut short and neat, his brown eyes warm. Dressed in civilian clothing, he wore an open-necked, checked shirt, revealing a smooth neck, and he was carrying his jacket over his arm.

As the Indian woman turned to leave, Jack stepped forward to the counter, and Donna was trapped. Squaring her shoulders, she lifted her chin defiantly.

'Hello, Donna,' Jack said. 'I've come to report a missing object.'

'You've come to the right place then.' Donna's voice answered tartly. 'What have you lost?'

'It's something very personal,' he said, raising his eyebrows.

'Oh, well, in that case,' she said, improvising rapidly, 'I'll pass you over to Natalia. I've got a meeting now.'

'What a shame,' he said. 'I was looking

forward to having your personal touch – no disrespect intended to you, Natalia. I'm sure you'll be great, especially as you've been trained by Donna.'

He was flirting with them. Donna tapped one manicured nail on the desk.

'Please, if there's anyone who can help me, it's you. I know that.'

Caught on the hop, Donna said, 'Very well, but as soon as the Area Commander arrives I'm going. Understood?'

'Same goes for me,' he replied, then leaned conspiratorially across the desk. 'So what are you two cooking up then, Mr Crane and Ms Harris?'

'Closer inter-departmental liaison,' Donna replied coolly.

'Oh, I see.' He smiled, flashing a look at Natalia that said, we know what she means by that, don't we? 'And what does that entail?'

'That's confidential information at the moment,' Donna replied. 'Look, Jack, have you really lost something or have you just come to annoy me?'

'Of course,' Jack replied, straightening up and turning professional. 'Your time is valuable, so is mine. It's my PDA – these ridiculous handheld computers we've got now instead of notebooks.'

'I know what a PDA is,' Donna said. 'I'll start a new file.' She began tapping at the computer keyboard, but carefully. She didn't often type for herself. Nor did she want to break a nail before Mr Crane arrived, Natalia thought. 'First of all, name and address.'

He recited an address in Bounds Green.

'OK. Description of item – it's OK, Jack, you don't need to say anything. Look here, Natalia, we can copy and paste a previous description of the same item.'

A couple of taps copied and pasted a general description of a personal handheld computer.

'I don't know, what with government secret documents left lying about on park benches and the private financial details of millions lost on buses, and now your PDA, I don't know how civil servants have become so careless.'

'I consider myself told off.'

'Did you personalise it at all?'

'I've got my serial number here.' Jack handed Donna a slip of paper, and she typed it in.

'Yours isn't the first to go missing,' she told him. 'And we've had several handed in over the past six months.'

'That's when they came down on us like a ton of bricks and insisted we start using them all the time. Damn things are more trouble than they're worth. Screen is hard to see, takes ages to type anything in.'

'What are they for?' Natalia asked. 'Do they make it easier to catch criminals? Do they give you information, like who a car belongs to, whether it's registered and so on?'

'That's generally the onboards. In the patrol cars. They're linked to central records. The PDA is mainly for writing up scenes of crime notes, stop and searches, that sort of thing. It's meant to revolutionise policing.'

While Donna began checking records to see if his PDA had been logged in, Natalia said, 'I suppose they save on paper and time.'

Jack shook his head. 'They're more trouble than they're worth. Besides, while we're standing there like computer nerds typing away, or using a touch pencil, the criminals are making a run for it. Or we're getting bogged down in the digital age while the victim is getting ignored.'

As Donna was still staring at the screen, Natalia asked, 'But surely they help you remember all the details more accurately, so you get more convictions?'

'A good policewoman or man should be able to handle all that already. Besides, it's like putting a screen between the police and the public they're trying to serve.' He cast a glance at Donna, whose eyes were still glued to the computer records.

'Got it,' she said. 'It's already put aside with some other London Underground and Transport Police items, ready to be returned to your headquarters in Westminster.'

'I'm glad it's here,' Jack said. 'But not glad it's going back to HQ. I'll get a right bollocking when they find out I lost it. Even though they're easy to lose.'

Donna looked sharply at him, then at Natalia. Natalia could almost hear the wheels turning in her head. Suddenly, Donna flashed a radiant smile.

'Tell you what. If you do me a favour, I'll do one for you.'

Natalia could swear she almost batted her eyelashes at him. He smiled warmly back.

'What can I do for you?'

'I will go and see if I can rescue your handheld, you won't have to sign for it, no questions asked – I'll delete this file. In return, Natalia has some concerns about some items found in – where was it?'

'Mornington Crescent.'

'I thought you'd know all there is to know about lost property,' Jack said gallantly.

'It's more than that. Natalia thinks women are being attacked there. She can explain, while I fetch your PDA from the vault.'

Donna slid gracefully away, leaving Jack and Natalia staring uncomfortably at one another. Natalia tried to recall the English expression for what Donna had just done. Hoodwinked, was that it? She knew Jack wasn't in a position to investigate something like this.

'Fire away then, Natalia. What's this all about?' he asked heartily.

But still, it was better to talk to him than say nothing. 'There seems to be a pattern,' she told him, proffering the sheets she had printed off. 'Items belonging to women, often damaged, turning up at about the same times. In restricted areas.'

Jack glanced at the papers. 'It'll be the heat, that's what it is, in my opinion. People trying to find places to get cool, most likely. Doing weird things when the heat goes to their heads. You wouldn't believe what Jason and me've seen on our Underground patrols. People taking their clothes off when it's sweltering at night. No wonder they're losing all these items.'

'But wouldn't someone notice if she'd lost her make-up bag? And why in private areas?'

'Well, Natalia, I've seen human nature at its best and at its worst. You wouldn't believe the crazy things people do, and this heat drives them even crazier. No one wants to stay indoors – no one can sleep at night anyway. The pubs and bars are doing a roaring trade, you must've noticed. And when people drink too much they fool about, or stagger about alone, not sure where they are. No way they're going to notice losing things.'

'I suppose so. But Mornington Crescent station. Why always there? Have you heard any reports of anything happening there?' She knew she was being fobbed off. First by Donna, and now by Jack. She could've asked Jason for this information, and she didn't need his mentor mentally assigning her the label of 'overactive imagination'. What she wanted was someone to set up an actual line of enquiry.

'I would've thought you were in the ideal position to see the sort of madness that's going on at the moment. Didn't I hear that a surfboard got left in the back of a taxi last week?'

'Yes, that's true.' But before she could pursue matters further, Avon bustled into reception.

'Detective Sergeant Jack Riley?' she asked in her most officious voice. 'Can I see some identification please?'

Jack raised his eyebrows but dutifully presented his warrant card.

'Very well. Out of the way, Natalia.' Avon pushed behind her and, breathing heavily, took over at the computer. 'I'm told you do *not* need to sign for this. Off the record, Donna said. So we won't be asking the usual twenty-pound fee for return of computer or electrical items.'

'Thank you very much, Avon, isn't it, if I remember right?' Jack was clearly amused at Avon's haughty attitude, but that changed when he picked up his PDA and switched it on.

'Seems OK,' he said, his thumbs working busily on the keypad. 'And all the info's still on there. I've got five Underground spot-check results to download back at the station.'

'I saw one last week,' Natalia said. 'Camden Town. What were you looking for? Drugs? Illegal immigrants?'

'Any kind of misdemeanour. If we uncover

something more serious, so much the better. We're not fussy.' He smiled at Avon, who coloured up. For one moment, Natalia thought she was going to ask him to institute a search for her lost hooter.

But they were disturbed by the sound of the doors opening. A tall, good-looking man entered and stood hesitating inside the door, his quick gaze taking them all in.

'Right,' Jack said. 'I'll be off. Sir,' he said, as he passed the newcomer and exited into the street.

Sir? Then this had to be–

'Jonathan!' Donna strode into reception, holding out her hand. She'd set her hair free from its restraining pin and had added more lip gloss.

Outside, Natalia saw Jack rapidly walking away, clearly not wanting a commanding officer questioning what he was doing at the LPO.

Jonathan Crane was worth the effort Donna had gone to in her appearance. His black hair was flecked with grey, cut short to his well-shaped head. Dark brows over dark-grey eyes, he was good-looking, clean shaven, with a well-shaped mouth.

He shook Donna's hand and looked around assessingly. A man who liked to take

81

control of his surroundings, Natalia thought, as his gaze returned to her for a second glance. She felt herself grow warm under his scrutiny. Avon's mouth was slightly open in wonder.

'Natalia, one of my staff,' Donna said. 'And this is my deputy, Avon. Would you like to come through to my office?'

'Why don't we talk over a cool drink?' he suggested.

Donna's face lit up. 'I know just the place–' she started.

Natalia stepped forward. 'Before you go,' she said. 'I want to tell you about a possible serial crime.'

'Oh yes?' the Area Commander became very still, watching her.

Behind him, Donna was shaking her head. 'Not now,' she mouthed.

Doggedly, Natalia told him, 'I've noticed that items of women's jewellery, or other personal belongings, keep turning up at Mornington Crescent station, at the same time of the week, but in a restricted area.'

'I see.' Jonathan Crane's expression was changing from one of interest to one of officialdom. Avon, clearly upset at not being the centre of attention, went back into the main office.

Natalia ploughed on. 'I think that women might be being attacked there somehow. One woman came here to claim her lost necklace. She could not remember what happened to her that night.'

'At British Transport Police, we take women's safety very seriously. We recognise that many women feel vulnerable when travelling alone, especially at night. I expect you've seen the circular, white help points positioned all over the Underground system now. These also contain a red emergency lever.'

'That wasn't quite what I–' Natalia started, ignoring Donna's furious glare.

'That's why we've increased the number of female officers, as well as the number of officers on foot patrol.'

'Yes, but I think–'

'And our policy is paying off. Despite the headlines – and I admit there's still much to do, especially relating to knife crime – overall crime is down several percentage points on London's public transport.' He turned to Donna. 'While we're not patting ourselves on the back yet, we certainly feel progress is being made.'

'I'm looking forward to hearing more,' Donna said, seizing the opportunity to lead him towards the exit.

Jonathan Crane paused and looked back. 'It's good to know that Donna's staff are vigilant. It's just the sort of extra help we need. Good night.' He nodded, but his face still wore its official expression, while the look Donna cast her was more of a scowl.

'That didn't go well,' Natalia muttered, as the doors closed behind them. Disconsolately she picked up the sheets of paper she'd printed off earlier. Was she mistaken? Should she consign them to the bin?

But reading it all through again, she felt the same certainty as before. Somehow, she had to find more evidence, so that she could convince Jonathan Crane, Jack – whoever – that something was seriously amiss. Before more women were put at risk.

6

It was the end of the working day, and Natalia headed out with Stefan, who was looking dressed up. They often travelled halfway together.

'Got a hot date tonight?'

'In truth, my date is with my computer. Time to catch up with the family through Skype. Seeing them on the screen makes it feel more like home. My grandfather is in hospital again.'

They headed for Baker Street station at a leisurely pace, Natalia enjoying its old-world charm, the shops, the old, wooden fascias before they reached the ticket barriers. Stefan lived in West Hampstead and sometimes she travelled on the Jubilee Line with him, changing there on to the Overground, which would take her to Hackney.

As she and Stefan clung on to a pole on the Jubilee Line, enduring the clammy heat, Stefan brought her up to date on his family, and she told him about hers in Poland.

'How much does your mother know about what you get up to?'

'She knows I go to church regularly – which I do – but there's no need to tell her everything...'

'And does she worry that you will meet a nice English girl and stay in this country for ever?'

'Probably. But she never says this. She doesn't want to put the idea into my head, I think.'

'And do you think you will meet someone

you can settle down with eventually?'

'Sure. When I'm eighty, I'm bound to be ready for a quiet life...'

Natalia gave him a playful prod in the chest, but the train lurched just as she did, sending him spiralling round the pole into the not insubstantial stomach of a pin-striped commuter.

'Perhaps a message from God,' Natalia quipped, laughing good-naturedly and helping him to his feet. 'That some girl's going to knock you off your feet.'

Reaching West Hampstead, the train emerged from the tunnel and rattled its way above ground. On either side, weeds and grass pushed their way through gravel and concrete, softening the cement wilderness. Graffiti was sprayed everywhere, telling a story that was hard for Natalia to decipher. She had read that some of the graffiti artists had become quite famous – notably one called 'Banksy'. She wondered whether she would recognise his work. Probably not, she thought.

The train pulled in at West Hampstead and they climbed out. Natalia was glad to feel fresh air on her skin. As they walked with the other passengers towards the exit stairs, Natalia shivered from head to toe.

Was it just the change of temperature, or was it an inkling of someone watching her? Even with Stefan beside her she was afraid to look round for fear of who she might see. But she made herself do it. It couldn't be Jem – surely – but if it was, that was the route to Paul. She had to be brave.

There were a handful of stragglers, and a woman in a straw hat and mac, sorting out her shopping bag resting on one of the seats. She felt a mix of relief and disappointment.

Still chatting, she and Stefan climbed the stairs, turning right. Although she knew she was not being followed, she still had the sensation of being watched. Looking around the station, Natalia caught sight of the CCTV cameras. That had to be it. What else could it be? They went through the barriers and exited onto the busy narrow road outside.

'Goodnight, Stefan,' she said, giving him a sisterly hug.

'Have a good evening, say hello to Dermot.' But then he hesitated. 'I'd like to ask your advice some time, Natalia,' he said.

'Is something troubling you?'

'Two things. One I think I've got under control. The other – you might be able to help me with.'

'Any time.'

They said goodnight again. Stefan crossed the road in long, loping strides, and Natalia turned right to walk along a row of shops before turning into the Overground station. She realised she no longer felt as if she were being followed.

What could be bothering Stefan? she wondered. Apart from concern for his grandfather, it seemed he lived a charmed life.

Natalia turned into the Overground under its flaming orange logo. There was no one about in the small hall. She bought a ticket from the automatic machine and went through the barriers, then headed for the stairs down to the platform. She heard a train just leaving the station, and then the unmistakeable sound of someone coming through the barriers behind her. For some reason, she quickened her pace, began to hurry down the stairs. She could not see anyone on the platform. Steps were running behind her now. Where was everyone?

Natalia stumbled and had to grab the handrail to steady herself She felt a body press into hers and had to stop herself gasping.

And then he was passing her by. A quick glance behind revealed a figure, dressed in black trousers and grey top, with the hood pulled low over his face. The hooded man paid her no attention as he ran past, hurtling down the steps and onto the platform. Natalia gasped with relief. Could it have been this young man she felt watching her earlier? She had not noticed him in particular. Perhaps he had skulked behind a pillar. But if he had deliberately followed her, he no longer seemed interested.

Or was he waiting for her on the platform? Natalia took the last few steps, looked up and down. He was at the farthest end, swaying slightly, talking to himself. She looked across. An older man with a bulging stomach was sitting on one of the benches, and a young woman was sitting with her iPod headphones on, feet tapping to the soundless music. At least she wasn't alone. And now she could hear someone coming down the stairs to her platform. She was safe now. How silly she had been to feel so anxious. All the same, she would be very glad to be held in Dermot's arms very soon.

7

Sitting opposite Rasheda in a Polish café around the corner from work, Natalia tucked into a bowl of iced borscht.

Rasheda had still not mentioned Raymond was coming out of prison, and what she was going to do about it. She'll tell me when she's ready, Natalia thought. She knows I'll do all I can to support her.

'I keep telling myself that Jem will have moved on, that the anger was part of that time when we were together. A toxic time. But some part of me is still anxious, afraid. After all, he is in England – he could be in London, walking the same streets I walk. Why London? Does he feel he hasn't punished me enough? He could have found out where I live, where I work and be watching me.' Natalia looked down at her soup, letting the purple liquid flow across her spoon. 'It's not something I want to talk to Dermot about. I don't want him to think I'm still hung up on my first husband, you see, and so–'

'And so you stop talking, because the thing you're not talking about is like a black hole, sucking everything else into it. Pow!' Rasheda said, nodding. The springy braids around her head bounced. Today they were restrained by a yellow headband, making her skin glow in contrast. She wore a matching yellow dress over her tall, ample figure.

'Exactly. And at the same time I want to make contact with Jem, because then I'll see Paul.' As always, the pleasure of being able to speak her son's name aloud brought a jolt of joy to her heart. 'Paul,' she said again, savouring his name. 'I just hate this feeling of fear.'

Rasheda delicately drank the last of her soup, keeping her spoon well away from her dress. 'Still no luck tracking him on the Internet, honey?'

Natalia shook her head. 'I've tried every avenue, from Turkish newspapers published in the UK, to websites and magazines about electronics. Very boring. But he was a very skilled worker. Maybe his name will come up.'

She too drank the last of her soup. The waitress saw they'd finished, topped up their wine and took their plates.

'Don't give up hope, honey.' Rasheda

squeezed Natalia's hand. 'You have to believe. Paul's out there and one day you'll see him again.'

'Thanks.' Natalia smiled. 'It's just Dermot was talking again the other day. About having a baby of our own. I want to, I really do, but then I think about Paul. It's putting more distance between us.' She chewed her lip, then drank some of the cold, dry white wine. 'I don't want to push him too far away, but how can I do something that feels wrong.'

'You'll know when the time is right. And Dermot is a good bloke. Maybe there'll come a time when you'll put him first?'

There was a wistful look in Rasheda's eyes. 'What is it?' Natalia asked. Would Rasheda choose to open up now, about her boys' father?

Rasheda sighed. 'There's so much going on, it's making my head spin. Where do I start? I just don't know which way to turn. Men! I ask you. What do they give us? Nothing but grief. Why do we put up with it?' She picked up her glass, upended it and drank half the wine inside, then put it down with a thump, the silver rings she always wore catching the light. 'Raymond is about to be released back into society, Gawd help us all. That's right, Ray, the father of my two boys. The bad penny.' Her fingers trembled where they touched the stem of the wine glass, Natalia saw. 'I don't know if it wouldn't have been better if he'd just disappeared, stayed out of all our lives. Plenty of men do that. Procreate, then move on. But not old Ray, uh-uh. He stickier than a sticky thing on sticky island,' she finished, exaggerating her Caribbean lilt. 'If only I didn't suspect – no, *know* – it's only 'cos he knows where he can get some good home cooking and a safe place to sleep for a while, before his next little adventure.'

They were interrupted by the arrival of their plates of cold herring, pickles, potato salad and a bowl of green salad to share. When the waitress had gone, Rasheda continued, 'I know I sound cynical, but that's what experience does for you.' Absent-mindedly, she broke up some bread on her side plate and began to eat it piece by piece.

'I don't remember you mentioning visiting him in prison.'

Rasheda shook her head vigorously. 'He told me not to. It's like he puts his mind to it, doing time, doesn't want no distractions. But this the longest time he been in. Two years. Sometimes he phones me, no good expecting it, or looking forward to it. I get a call, maybe two, out of the blue, then nothing for months.'

'I suppose it's the same for you. He's doing his time, you're doing yours, getting on with your life,' Natalia observed.

'That's just it! I've got my routine, my life's in order. I've got my job, my friends. I've got the boys' lives together. I've got Jason through his exams and doing the job he loves, and now Daniel – well, maybe he won't do so well, not unless he chooses to. He's such a contrary kid.'

'You've done all you can, working extra shifts to pay for extra tuition. It's up to him now.'

Rasheda swallowed her mouthful of salad. 'The last thing that boy needs is his so-called father unsettling him. Oh why did he have to get time off for good behaviour?'

Natalia put down her knife and fork. 'I think Ray will be unsettling you, too.'

'Oh, I'm well over him. Look, Daniel's fifteen. In all those years Ray has spent as much time inside as he has out, and when he's out, sometimes he knocks on my door, sometimes he doesn't. Well, I'm not having it any more. My door is staying firmly closed. At least it would, if only–' She trailed off, looking at Natalia.

'If only you didn't think that maybe it would be good for the boys to see their father?'

'Jason's never had any problem with it. You know him. He takes the rough with the smooth and can laugh off most things. It's Daniel I'm worried about. That boy takes everything to heart so much. If I let Ray back in – to my house if not my bed – what sort of role model is he going to be? Supposing Daniel says, my dad doesn't give a stuff about exams, so why should I?'

'But if you turn him away and Daniel finds out, he'll be very upset and who knows what he'll do then?'

'Damned if you do–'

'And damned if you don't!'

They clinked glasses and Natalia continued eating, listening as Rasheda rambled on about Ray. For all her protestations that she had no space for him in her heart, or her bed, Natalia could also see the flush in her cheek, the light in her eye. He still held a fascination for her. With his ability to sweet talk, she wondered what chance her friend had against his beguiling ways.

They didn't have time to try the delicious torte, a speciality of this little Polish café

Natalia had found, so after a quick coffee, they paid the bill and left.

'Back to work now,' Natalia said, as they stood in the tiny bit of shade cast by the building, in air thick with heat. 'I expect Avon will be pleased I'm late, so she can put another black mark against my name. She's got so many against me, she'll have to start another book soon.'

'That woman still on your case?'

'She's on everyone's case – it's what she does, Mark says. And of course she is not talking to anyone, not until the culprit owns up who has taken her hooter. The thief started sending her emails with photos of the thing all over London. Can you believe that? So now she knows it was one of us, she's been if more impossible. The latest one she was sent by the hooter kidnapper had the caption: "Hooter on a scooter", and came with a picture of it driving past Harrods. She gets one every day. I wonder what today's will be?'

'Tiny minds,' groaned Rasheda. 'Tiny minds. Amazing what you can do with a computer these days, though. You can fake most anything. I have to go and do some shopping now. Jason wants a new shirt.'

They embraced and kissed each others'

cheeks and turned away, when Natalia had a sudden thought. 'Oh, Rasheda,' she called after her friend's departing back. 'Can I ask you something?'

Rasheda heard her. 'What is it?'

'Do you happen to know any of the cleaners who go down into the Underground stations to clean at night? Or know someone who knows them?'

'They're a different crew, but if I ask around I might come across someone I've worked with, yes. Why?'

'Mornington Crescent. Know anyone who's worked down there recently?'

'Not offhand, but I can ask around.'

'Thanks. Let me know if you find out!'

8

Natalia walked slowly through the intense early afternoon heat. Smells intensified, she caught a whiff from a sweaty passer-by, a large man whose shirt was wet through, and then a fatty tang from a burger-bar kitchen outlet caught her throat, making her gag. The heat was changing people, too, and not for the better.

Faces of Londoners were strained, tempers fraying easily. Over the road, a middle-aged woman in a linen suit was yelling at a lycra-clad cyclist who'd ignored a red light and run over her toe. Several folk had gathered round, joining in on either side. And right beside her, the driver of a bus pulled up at a stop was involved in an angry altercation with a young woman carrying a child.

'You should've stopped at that bus stop – now I've got to walk all the way back.'

'It's a request stop. You didn't press the bell.'

'Since when has it been a request stop. I always get off there. You just didn't want to stop.'

'You've got it wrong, lady. It's a request stop and no one pressed the bell.'

'We'll see about that. I'm checking and I'm going to report you.'

'Get off my bus, you're holding up other passengers.'

The passengers were on the side of the young woman.

'She's got to walk back now, in all this heat, carrying the child. You should've stopped.'

The bus driver raised his weary shoulders.

The doors folded closed with a hiss and a bang.

Natalia entered the office expecting to be met by a steely glare from Avon making a great show of tapping her watch with a red-taloned finger. But Avon was nowhere to be seen. Natalia glanced over at Donna's office. The door was open but she too was missing. Rose glanced up, as if sensing Natalia's gaze, and smiled briefly before returning to her work. There was something different about her today. Was it her hair? No, her neat bob of brown hair was unchanged. She wore the same sensible, though not outdated, clothes. Perhaps she was wearing a little make-up today, that was it. And then Natalia saw the box of chocolates on her desk. Another gift from her secret admirer.

Maybe Avon and Donna were in a meeting together. That would put Donna's deputy in a good mood. She liked nothing better than her boss giving her special status and responsibility. As she reached her desk, Natalia caught Mark watching her expectantly, a smile on his face.

On her keyboard was a sheet of paper showing an illustration. It was Avon's hooter on its travels again. The hooter was at a bar in a pub. The caption at the bottom read:

'Hooter meets a publican'. She smiled back at Mark. 'How did you get this?'

'Waited for Avon to leave the office just now, then printed it off her computer. You should've heard her when she opened the email a little while ago. Don't know if she was madder at the idea of her hooter buying a drink, or at not knowing who's sending them.'

Natalia narrowed her eyes. 'Mark, it's not you, is it?'

He assumed an innocent expression. 'Do I look the sort of geezer'd do a thing like that?'

'You look exactly the sort of–'

'It's not me. I haven't got that much imagination and computer savvy.'

'Maybe not. But remember I,' she pointed at herself, then her eyes, 'am watching you.' She pointed at him.

They both laughed. Avon threatened her staff in just such a way. Natalia looked again at the composite photo, before crumpling it up and throwing it in the wastepaper bin. Mark had a point. His head was filled with football, and probably cricket now the summer season had started. She'd heard him mentioning such incomprehensible things as 'silly mid on' and 'square leg', not to mention 'leg byes' as he tried to explain the game to Stefan. Without success.

She felt an unexpected twinge for Avon. It was too easy to wind her up. That was the trouble. She flew off the – what was it – the handle? – at the smallest thing. On the other hand, these emails – 'The Hooter Diaries' Mark called them – were gentle humour and quite creative in their own way. She could almost imagine Avon's hooter, liberated from the Lost Property Office, enjoying its adventures around London.

A loud crash, followed by some swearing and then Cliff's measured tones, made everyone's heads fly up. It was Avon and Cliff, emerging from the vault together. So that was where she'd been. Between them they were carrying a large, wooden chest. Avon was red-faced and panting, shouting commands at Cliff as she backed into the office, succeeding in banging the chest against an empty desk.

'What the–?' And why wasn't Stefan helping Cliff carry it?

'Steady now, lassie,' Cliff said.

Natalia marvelled at Cliff's composure. He worse his habitual dour expression, but his tone and his eyes were kindly.

'OK, forward to me, then bear to your left – no *your* left–' *Clang!* 'That's it. Steady as

101

you go.'

But then Avon was distracted by the sight of Stefan arriving from the entrance to the vault, and suddenly Avon was shrieking at the top of her voice, 'Hold on, you're going to—'

Cliff, caught by surprise, was unable to hold it.

Crash!

The chest fell on the floor. It teetered on one end for a moment then tipped over. The lid flew open, the contents of the chest spilling out.

'It's the Dildo Drawers,' Natalia thought she heard Mark say. Surely not – but looking towards the floor, there was no denying it.

Natalia saw a strange jumble of leather straps, gleaming buckles, wispy see-through gauze, riding crops, unnameable rubber objects – and the dildos themselves. Da-glo pink, fluorescent yellow, pink, with ridges and bumps, and of sizes either mouthwatering or eye-watering depending on your preference.

'I suppose that's one way to find your hooter,' Mark crowed, as Avon and Cliff dropped to their knees, hurriedly scooping up the offending items.

'Why you–' Avon cried, exasperated.

Everyone stood up and congregated around the contents of the chest. Even Rose joined them, holding her hand over her mouth, eyes meeting Natalia's with an amused gleam.

The chest in which the sex aids mislaid on public transport were kept was now locked away. Previously they had been kept in the locked Special Items room, its secret known only to Cliff and Donna, but Donna had decided that it was time to modernise, and the room was now a storage space for the most expensive items brought in – from electrical equipment to jewellery – and the 'naughty things', as Ranjiv called them, were locked in the chest. Only Avon and Donna had keys to the chest. Why not Cliff? Natalia wondered.

'Here, lassie, let's get this tidied up.' Practical Cliff was already bending over to straighten the chest, stepping gingerly over its contents, then beginning to pick up items that looked strangely small in his big fists, and passing them to Avon. She snatched them from his grasp and moved quickly away, as if he was on fire. 'All right, all right,' she snapped. 'I can manage.'

'Och, have it your own way, lassie.' Cliff dropped the item he was holding – a vibrator decorated, for some inexplicable reason, in tartan – on the floor. His brows beetling down over his eyes, he said, 'If you'd listened to me in the first place, none of this would've happened. Stefan could've helped me.'

He stomped over to Natalia, who made space for him, and stood beside her, arms folded over his barrel of a chest. He sounded snarly, but Natalia had seen behind his craggy mask that he was really a sweetheart, and recognised that he'd been hurt by Avon's reaction. She hadn't wanted him close to her. But why? He'd only wanted to help.

At that very moment, Natalia heard Donna's frosty voice. 'What in heaven's name is going on in here? It doesn't take all of you to tidy up – Avon, sort it out will you, please?'

Natalia looked round. Donna rarely used such an icy tone, preferring irony, but the reason was immediately apparent. Beside her stood the dishy Jonathan Crane. He was staring at the items still scattered on the floor with a bemused expression.

'But ... but ... I was just...' Avon began to

splutter an explanation.

Donna refused to listen. 'Come along, Jonathan, come into my office. Rose, fetch us some tea, please.'

'Exit one furious Donna,' Natalia said to Cliff, as they moved away. 'I think that's the maddest I've ever seen her.'

'Aye, well, it's promotion she's after.'

'Of course.' Natalia nodded. 'Is she intending to leave us?'

'Mebbe. It's one of the nonsense jobs that the guys upstairs dream up. Chief Liaison Officer and being assigned to the Metropolitan Police. Based at New Scotland Yard no less. I've no doubt she's after the post, another rung up the ladder – or the greasy pole, if you prefer.'

'Ah ha.' Natalia nodded again. Cliff had Donna's measure as much as she did.

'She'd want to look good in front of Mr Crane there,' he jerked his head in the direction of Donna's office, where they could see her blonde head and his dark one bent together. 'Though if she really wanted to impress him, she'd do better explaining the rules of Mornington Crescent to him. Eh?' Laughing, he dug her in the ribs with his elbow. 'The rules of Mornington Crescent, eh?' Chuckling and shaking his head he walked off towards the vault.

The rules of Mornington Crescent? What on earth was Cliff talking about?

9

'Come on, Nuala, you can't keep borrowing money like that to build more hotels.' Dermot's exasperated voice rang across their living room, penetrating Natalia's single-minded focus on the bright screen of her laptop in front of her.

'Dad, it's called Monopoly. It's only a game.' Nuala had perfected her teenage tone of bored forbearance in the face of what was to her, blatant parental stupidity.

'Come on, No-oola. Come on, No-oola.' Connor set up a football chant softly in the background.

'Natalia, back me up here, will you? Nuala's supposed to save money to buy, not keep looking for loans, surely.'

Nuala stuck her tongue out at her dad, who stuck his out back again. Giggling, Connor stuck his out, too, and blew a very wet raspberry.

'Watch out, Connor, you've made the board all wet,' Nuala said.

'Natalia, what d'you say?'

'Hmmm?' Natalia dragged her eyes away from the screen and looked over to Dermot. The three of them had pushed back the coffee table and the old, battered Monopoly board was positioned on the brightly coloured rug between their settee, the television and an armchair. Dermot lay on his side, head propped up in his hand. He was wearing his oldest jeans and a short-sleeved, white shirt, emphasising the blackness of his thick, curly hair, flecked here and there with grey.

Nuala sat cross-legged. She wore a pair of very tight, blue jeans, with a wide, white belt, and a purple-and-white loose top. Her thick, black hair was straight and glossy, and the make-up, which she put on as soon as she came out of school, was immaculate and understated.

She could give me lessons on applying my make-up, Natalia thought.

On the other side of the board, Connor was lying on his stomach, head propped up in both hands, feet waving in the air. He was wearing just a pair of khaki Bermuda shorts. He hummed happily to himself, not mind-

107

ing when he got the rules wrong, just enjoying being part of the game. What a sunny child, she thought, like my nephew, Tomas. Maybe they will meet one day...

'Natalia!' Dermot called out again. 'What do you think? You know, this game would be much more fun if *four* were playing.'

'I promise I'll join in next time. Then you'd better watch out!'

'Are you good at Monopoly?' Connor asked.

'She's terrible,' Dermot said. 'But she gets all the good luck.'

Natalia returned her attention to the computer screen, feeling Dermot's eyes still on her. But this was her daily ritual now. Surely he would not mind if she spent just a few more minutes in her search before she joined them.

In front of her was one of the online newspapers of the Turkish community in the United Kingdom. Some were only posted once a week, but there were daily newsletters, too. Some were in English, some in Turkish. She had attended Turkish language evening classes for a while, but Jem had been more interested in learning Polish and English, and wanted to practise these with her, so she'd given the lessons up. She understood a few words, but mainly she was looking for names. His name. And pictures. She still lived in hope that one day his or Paul's photograph would jump out at her.

She also liked to Google his name, in case that yielded results. However, once again and with a heavy heart, she had to admit defeat. Her tireless searches had not brought any information to light as to his whereabouts – and the whereabouts of Paul – in the United Kingdom. She didn't even know if they were in England, Wales, Scotland or Northern Ireland. All Fatima had said was Jem has taken Paul to the UK, and since then he'd only communicated with his family from internet cafés and had given no clues to his family about where he was living.

'You all right, Natalia?' It was Dermot again. She realised she must have sighed.

'I'm logging off now,' she told him. 'I'm not getting anywhere today.'

'Dad, Dad, watch out, you're pushing my racing car off the board!' Connor punched his dad playfully on the hand.

Dermot responded by rough housing Connor for a moment, while Nuala disdainfully kept her distance.

Natalia hesitated, hand on mouse. She

109

had hoped to have a moment to follow up on what was to her, her well-founded suspicion that vulnerable women were being assaulted at Mornington Crescent station. But she sensed that Dermot wanted her to spend time with him and his children. And he was right to think that, of course.

She clicked the mouse. The screen on her laptop went dead, and she closed the lid.

'Am I going to have to be umpire or referee?' she said, standing over the trio.

'You can take my place if you like, Natalia,' Nuala said in her most grown-up voice. 'I want to text my friends.'

'You'll stay right where you are, young lady,' Dermot ordered. 'And we'll play a game together, all four of us.'

Nuala hunched her shoulders with a small pout, but she remained where she was. They had negotiated text-free periods of time, and Natalia saw Dermot's point. If she stayed on the Internet, it would undermine their efforts to have some time spent eating and playing together without outside distractions. At first, there had been grumbles and whining from both of them about giving up computer-based games, listening to music on the iPod, and communicating with friends. But Dermot and Natalia had stood firm and the children seemed genuinely to enjoy quality time with them now, however old the games were they played.

Their lives are so pressured these days, Natalia mused looking down at one auburn head, one black. They have to be so stylish, so cool, so young. And the danger on the streets of London was evident in stabbings and deaths every week. Was it more dangerous here or in Baghdad? At least they had these safe moments when they could just relax and be children. Though sometimes she wondered whether Nuala was just acting out another one of her parts, and whether her bullying tendencies still lurked under the surface. If they were, she hoped they would vanish when the worst of her teenage years were over.

The doorbell sounded. 'I'll go,' Natalia said. 'You'd better be ready for me when I come back, though!'

Sunil and Araminda stood outside, Natalia and Dermot's immediate neighbours on the fourth-floor landing. Sunil wore dark trousers and a blue shirt with a woollen pullover on top, despite the heat. His wife wore a swathing yellow-and-red sari. She carried a precious bundle wrapped up in a shawl.

'Your baby is so beautiful!' Natalia exclaimed, peeping inside the shawl and seeing a tiny sleeping face with a wisp of black hair. 'How is he? Would you like to come in?'

She had watched Araminda toiling up and down the stairs of their building, suddenly huge in the last month of pregnancy, and walking gingerly on the icy streets outside in January and February. When their baby boy had been born in early March, relatives had seemed to swarm the stairs every day, some flying in from Sri Lanka to see the new arrival. Now the visitors had reduced to normal levels.

'Look, everyone.' She led them into the living room. 'It's Sunil and Araminda with their new baby.'

'Oh, you are playing game,' Sunil said. 'Please, go on.'

After shaking his hand, Dermot said, 'We're at the crucial point, it'll all be over in a matter of moments. Nuala's about to crumble.'

'Dad! I am so, *not*.'

Sunil and Araminda sat down on the sofa. As Natalia busied herself with getting drinks and snacks out, helped by Dermot, she saw how Araminda's eyes barely left the face of her sleeping baby. Araminda spoke little English as yet, but her dark eyes were filled with such fierce love, pride and wonderment that words were not necessary. She saw Nuala come over and look down at the baby, reaching out a tentative finger to stroke his rounded cheeks.

Connor took a glance at the child. 'Cool!' he said, and then was soon absorbed in his latest superhero comic.

'Please, play this game,' Sunil said. 'I want to see how British play.'

Natalia joined the others on the floor. Dermot rousted Connor out from his comic. They chose their pieces, and one round had been played when the phone rang. This time, Dermot answered, giving Connor and Nuala a chance to fool about, moving their pieces to advantage over his.

'Harika,' he said, returning and handing the handset to Natalia. She scrambled to her feet, and went to the open window, stuffing a finger in her ear to shut out Dermot's protests at his children's 'cheating' accompanied by Sunil's laughter.

'Hello, Harika, how are you?'

'I am well, and you? Children are good, I can hear!'

'Nothing wrong with them, that is true.'

Over the months since Christmas, Natalia felt she had built the foundations of a friendship with Harika at the Turkish Centre in north London. She had given her only the barest of facts about her marriage break up, when asking for her help in looking out for news of Jem and Paul. Partly because she still felt somehow ashamed, as if she was to blame for him turning on her so violently. And partly for the sake of her first husband and child. Jem might have changed, he might not, but telling the world their private business would only serve to alienate him, when she wanted to draw him in, if that was the only way to have contact one day with Paul.

'You have news for me?' she asked, keeping the desperation from her voice.

'Not today, Natalia, I'm sorry. That lead I was following for you turned out to be nothing. But I want you to know, I am still working on it. Within the Turkish community I can send out feelers, keep my ear to the ground. We will be successful, I am sure.'

'Thank you.'

As she turned around, she met Dermot's eyes. She gave a slight shake of her head. And then Araminda and Sunil's baby woke up and began to cry.

Later, much later, Natalia sat leaning against Dermot in front of the television, both their pairs of feet nestling on the same footstool. Sunil and Araminda had left some time ago. The ten o'clock news was on, and both children were in bed, in one case – Connor's – possibly even asleep. On the occasional nights they stayed over, Dermot would lay out breakfast before he left and Natalia would make sure they caught the right transport to get them to school in time in the morning.

As the newscaster spoke about turbulent weather in other parts of the world, Natalia noticed her necklace. Three strands of gem-stones. I wonder if that is a family heirloom and is as precious to you as Polly's is to her, she mused. She had not been able to spend any more time on the Internet looking for evidence to back up her suspicions about assaults on women, but now another thought occurred to her.

'Dermot.'

'Uh huh.'

'I think I might give Omar a ring. It's not too late is it?'

'What're you wantin' to be ringing him now for?'

'Well, it's what I was telling you about. Mornington Crescent. I must find more evidence and even though he's been promoted to senior position, maybe he can let me look at some CCTV footage.'

'And you think you'll find what all those experts he has under him haven't noticed?' Dermot shifted irritably away from her.

'If women are being assaulted, and the cameras have not recorded it, there must be a reason. I want to find out.'

'Oh, for heaven's sake, Natalia, can't we have a few moments together without your mind going off somewhere else!' Dermot said, thumping the seat of the settee in frustration.

Natalia blinked. She'd set off one of his rare explosions of hot temper. But why?

'I won't be long on the phone with Omar,' she said. 'I just want to make an appointment with him if I can. Why are you angry?'

'What the hell, make your call. I'm tired. I think I'll go to bed.'

Natalia stared after his retreating back. That must be it. He was exhausted after a long day at the site, with the constant knowledge of the deadlines for the Olympic locations to be ready on time for 2012, and in all this heat, too. And having a crying baby in the house...

Could that be it? Had the proximity of such a young baby stirred up his emotions again, and his resentment towards her for resisting his gentle pressure to have a baby had boiled over?

Natalia switched the television off, secured the windows for the night, and took one last look around the living room before turning off the lights. Until now this room, this home, had held nothing but joy for her. Tonight, as so many times recently, it had been the scene of a family enjoying themselves together. This was just a blip. Dermot was tired, and she would put him first. She'd phone Omar in the morning.

Everything would be all right between her and Dermot by then.

10

'Over here, Natalia. I'm over here.'

Passing through the security check barrier at Bank station a few days later, Natalia heard her name being called out. A tall, lean man headed towards her. It was Omar, a man with more than fifteen years' experience in London Transport's CCTV security.

'Thanks for agreeing to see me on such short notice.'

'This way,' he ordered, ushering Natalia towards the grey metal bank of lifts, standing aside to allow her to enter first.

He was still so oddly formal with her, she thought. How much it was part of his culture, and how much the nature of the man himself, she was never sure.

Swiping his security clearance card to activate the lift, they descended into the nerve centre of London Transport's CCTV headquarters, in the ancient heart of the City of London, the city within a city. The headquarters were Omar's domain.

'That's new since I was here last,' Natalia said, pointing at the card.

Last Christmas, Omar had helped her track down something larger than the average item that comes into the LPO. A missing person; Helen Bookman. Thanks to his skills, Natalia had been able to get to her in the nick of time, and prevented her from committing suicide.

'Security seems to get tighter and tighter. I don't suppose you've changed your mind about that job I offered you?'

'I do think about it from time to time,' Natalia admitted. 'But I'm still enjoying all the stories from the world of lost objects too much. That sense of satisfaction when you reunite object with owner – the reconnection. It still gives me a buzz.'

'If you do change your mind, let me know. It can be equally fulfilling tracking someone on CCTV, as you know.'

'I do, and I haven't forgotten all your training. It was a fascinating experience.'

Even though they'd shared an office for only a couple of weeks before Christmas, when Omar had been virtually ostracised, his teaching had been very thorough. She was grateful she'd learned the basics of CCTV surveillance from one of the most skilled operators in the business. At the time, Omar had been cool and distant, trusting no one, least of all this stranger who'd been foisted on him. But gradually he'd thawed. Now she and Dermot counted him and his wife Jamila among their friends.

Exiting the lift, overhead lighting hummed behind grey panels. Omar walked with a long, loose stride. Natalia hurried to keep up, her loose, flowered skirt floating out around her ankles as she walked, struck by the oppressiveness of the tunnel walls closing in around her. It took a different breed of person to her to handle that environment every day. She needed light and air and warmth. Down here, with no windows and no glimpse of the sky, the atmosphere felt distorted. It was charged with an intense energy she couldn't place her finger on.

Omar pressed his security code into a keypad, pushed open the heavy, metal door, and they entered into the vast arena of CCTV computer consoles that was CCTV HQ.

Natalia paused before entering, again struck by the contrast to her own offices, where there was always the greater hum of banter and laughter above the machines.

Hundreds of personnel sat concentrating on flickering stop-motion images as they scanned London's transport system for problems, trouble, breakdowns and violence. The room was a functional space, with metal piping and tubing above, grey carpet tiles, nothing of a personal nature. Above, watching over all, the glassed-in command centre, jutting out like the flight deck of a spaceship. One of the most senior commanders of this team, that was where Omar usually spent his days.

But for now he was happy to be back at a

computer screen, checking through the flickering images.

'Pull up a seat, Natalia,' Omar invited, as Natalia squeezed in beside him and another operator, oblivious even to Natalia's presence, so focused as he was on his work.

'What would you like to look for, Natalia?' he asked.

'Mornington Crescent station from, say, nine o'clock in the evening to the early hours. Starting on Friday, two weeks ago.'

'Ah, the famous station,' Omar said but, before she could ask him what he meant, he said, 'Sit down here, and let's see how much you remember. I'd better check what the security codes are for running that old tape.'

Natalia sat down and Omar leant over beside her, his slender fingers expertly manipulating the mouse. 'Although,' he said, 'There's something about that station – I can't quite remember what – ah, here it is, May the 23rd. That's the northbound platform, next stop Camden Town, that's the southbound, next stop King's Cross. And this one...' He pointed to the split screen. 'Is at the entrance, this one for the stairs. We have to check the lifts separately.' They watched the screen for a while, familiarising themselves with the norm.

121

'Anything particular we should be looking for?' he asked.

'A woman in her mid-twenties with wild, brown, corkscrew curls. Average height. I'll know her when I see her.'

'I'll speed it up and jump forward, see if we can get a fix on the time.'

Omar ran forward through Friday evening, the figures on the screen racing to and fro at top speed until, suddenly, at eleven, the screens went completely blank, one by one.

'What the–' Omar exclaimed, before calling across to the man sitting by Natalia's side. 'Smithy, you cover the Camden region. Know anything about the monitors going down at Mornington Crescent?'

The man swivelled around in his seat. An owlish man, Natalia was struck by the irony of how this man could stare so intently at his machine, but could barely bring himself to look Omar square in the eye.

'They're c-carrying out some m-maintenance work at Mornington Crescent on the electrical systems,' he stuttered, 'which means they switch off the CCTV cameras.'

'Ah, I remember now,' Omar nodded, before turning back to Natalia.

Natalia stared at the blank screen,

disappointed, her imagination wondering.

'It must be very eerie down there at night with no passengers and no trains running. Just miles of endless black tunnels spreading out like a web underneath London...'

'I've heard tell of plenty of ghost stories.' Omar smiled. 'Those tunnels are cut through all the layers of London's history from before Roman times. This city's foundations consist of at least thirty feet of rubble and tools and goodness knows what of all the previous centuries. But I can assure you, Natalia, I've never seen a ghost on the CCTV, nor have any of us here.'

'Perhaps they don't show up on man-made installations?' she suggested, grateful to Omar for taking her thoughts in another direction.

'The only thing we see is the wildlife. Rats and mice, the occasional pigeon, some-times–'

A thought struck Natalia. 'That means there are electricians working at that station at midnight onwards.'

Omar agreed. 'Would you like to watch the footage again of that evening?'

'I would. There aren't any cameras covering the fire-exit tunnels are there? The lost items were found in that restricted area, not out on the main platforms.'

'I'll take a look, but I doubt it.'

Omar drew up a chair, folded his long limbs and sat down. Heads bent together, they studied the footage for half an hour, without success. Eventually, frustrated, Natalia said, 'I mustn't keep you any longer. We're not going to see anything on there.'

They stood up.

'How are the children, and Jamila,' she asked, wanting to get back to normality and shake off this dreadful feeling of foreboding she felt.

'Jamila is very well. And the baby walked right across the room yesterday without any help, before collapsing on her bottom. And your two?'

'They're real good. Nuala spends all her spare time at singing and drama lessons. Having a purpose has transformed her. She sometimes speaks a whole sentence instead of just grunting. It really helps now that her mother spends girl time with her. As for Connor, he's still no trouble. He's getting his dad into judo now. They go to classes together. When are you two coming to see us again?' she asked.

'Soon, I hope. I must show you,' Omar said, reaching into his back jeans pocket for his wallet. 'Some new photos of the children. It's a few weeks since you saw them. See how my son has grown. He's doing very well at school. He loves it. Here he is in the back garden with a football.'

Natalia felt a sharp pang of loss as she looked at the photo. That last photo of Paul showed him standing in the back garden of wherever it was he lived in Turkey, in a Manchester United strip, holding a football and squinting into the sun. Almost immediately she was annoyed with herself for letting her defences fall.

Beside her, Omar stopped talking. He simply put his long arms around her and folded her into a hug, understanding only too well the pain of separation. Natalia stared down at his thick, tooled leather belt, his white shirt tucked in. She knew the story of that belt now. When Omar, his wife and two children had been forced to leave Iran – they'd subsequently had a baby since arriving in England – he'd left his brother behind. This was his brother's belt. He'd sworn to wear it every day until they were reunited. If his brother survived his time in the Iranian army.

'He's all the family I have left, now my mother and father are dead. He is my link with the past,' he'd told her in one of their moments of shared understanding. He knew she had lost her son, Paul. One day, Omar, she said to herself, you and I will find our missing loved ones and be reunited.'

'Thank you, Omar. And if you hear anything about Mornington Crescent at all, could you let me know?'

'I will.'

Natalia started to rise, then sat down again. 'There is one other thing – I can check for myself if you have to go.'

Omar shook his head. 'I have plenty of time,' he told her. 'I'm my own boss now.'

'Just five days ago, I was at West Hampstead station – between seven and half-past. Stefan and I went home together on the Jubilee Line after work.'

'Someone came after me – I'm sure he was watching me when we got off the Underground. It was all very strange.'

Images of Jem flashed before her mind.

'We'll soon find out what you look like on camera.'

She was conscious of Smithy's fingers slowing down, watching Omar's screen, and shifted around uncomfortably, the thought of who could be watching you at any given moment making her skin itch.

Natalia saw Stefan first. 'Oh look, there we are, getting off the train. Oh, yes, and there's that woman with the funny sun hat. I remember seeing her on the platform.' She leaned forward and looked very carefully. 'But I don't see any young lad in a hood.'

'I'll follow you forward and up the stairs.'

She watched herself and Stefan move along the platform and start up the stairs. When they came to the top they passed close to a camera. Omar flicked onto the next camera, outside the barriers, but Natalia clutched his arm.

'Go back, go back!' she said excitedly.

He flicked back. Natalia and Stefan again passed the camera, and so did another person.

'Can we enlarge there? Zoom in on that face?'

'I can try, but we don't want to go too close or the pixels break down.'

The camera went closer once, twice and then Natalia clapped a hand to her mouth, turning to Omar.

'I see who it is now. I knew there was something that looked very familiar.'

11

'One thousand slash A2,' Natalia muttered aloud to herself, reading from the docket in her hand and looked up again at the row upon row of handbags. Dull, olive-green floor-to-ceiling shelving stretched either way as far as the eye could see. Shelves laden with every kind of item, all grouped neatly according to type, and each with a neat, brown label attached by string, bearing its unique reference number.

When she'd first ventured into the Lost Property Office's vault, led by Cliff McDougall himself, it had appeared to go on into infinity. More accustomed to it now, it seemed to have shrunken in size and she knew more or less where each category of items was held. But the sheer variety of objects that humankind carelessly left behind still entranced and amazed her. Here she was in the handbag section, where everything from the most shabby and worn leather, or cheap plastic, rubbed shoulders with designer labels such as Burberry and

Armani. They all sat side by side on the shelves. There was no class distinction here.

Next to them were purses and wallets. All had had their contents carefully counted, checked and double-checked in case of cash and credit cards. Every detail recorded in Sherlock. Left unclaimed after three months, then the items were sent to auction and the money donated to charity. In the case of shoes, they'd started their own system of donating direct to the homeless who lived on the streets of London.

Further on was the cascade of umbrellas of every size and type, from child's plastic to furled black with ornate, wooden handles. Clothes from outer wear to underwear. School satchels, children's lunchboxes and pencil cases. The shoes were Avon's favourite section though. She often lingered there, checking to see if there were any Jimmy Choos in, which she could caress and covet.

Books came next, the most frequently lost item. Natalia often found herself stopping to browse the shelves, always ahead of the curve on what was the latest fad. Then there were the walking sticks, crutches, false limbs and eyes, wigs – and even plaster casts. As for the false teeth, she always rushed past them, as if they might suddenly nip her.

She could imagine, having seen the film *Toy Story* recently, curled up on the sofa with Connor, all the inhabitants of the vault coming to life after Cliff had done his final rounds, switched off the lights, and locked the metal grille at the entrance. But every morning, each item was back in its rightful place.

Except for 1000/A2, she thought, scratching her head. And where was Cliff? She was used to Stefan disappearing and never being where he was needed. She had, in fact, passed him on his way out as she'd entered the vault. Instead of stopping to chat, however, he'd grinned sheepishly and hurried on his way, no doubt to indulge in a cigarette outside in the heat and dust of Baker Street. It showed how addicted he – and Cliff – must be not to mind the discomfort outside, as long as they could get their nicotine fix.

Where had Cliff got to? She paused and listened. She couldn't hear him moving about. His shoes were silent, but you could often hear the rattling of the shelves or the swish of a brush. She looked around and her eye lighted on the door which was still labelled 'No Entry'. That was where all the sex aids and sex equipment handed in used to be, kept under lock and key. But Donna deemed it a hangover from a more prudish past and had turned it into a storage area for laptops and other expensive electrical equipment, as well as jewellery.

Could Cliff be in there? Having a crafty fag? Surely not. But maybe item 1000/A2 was hiding in there.

'Ouch!'

Natalia rubbed her shin, which had collided painfully with a large, wooden box. Who had put that there? It was the sex-aids chest that Avon had dropped the other day right in front of British Transport Police Area Commander, Jonathan Crane. Donna had had a few sharp words to say to Avon after that. 'If you want to check the contents, do it in the vault, not out here,' Natalia had heard her say.

Consequently, Avon had taken it out on the rest of them. In particular, continuing to interrogate each of them in turn as to the whereabouts of her lost hooter. Today's email had shown it standing in front of the Houses of Parliament: 'Hooter makes a vote'. Avon had not been amused.

I'd better tell Cliff that the chest is blocking an aisle, she thought. It was unlike him not to tidy it away properly. It had been unlocked when Avon brought it out. She tested the lid. Still unlocked. She thought about looking inside, but at the moment she and Dermot did not seem to need any extra help. On second thoughts, she left it closed.

Opening the door, Natalia was confronted with the sight of Cliff, sitting on a camping chair, a magazine open on his lap.

'Cliff! I've been looking for you,' she began, then watched in horror as, in his hurry to drop the magazine and stand up, Cliff slowly toppled backwards in an undignified heap.

'Let me help you.' Natalia stepped forward to grasp his arm and help him up.

Cliff, however, pushed her away. Looking red and embarrassed he scrambled to his feet.

'I can get myself up,' he growled. 'Why didn't you knock? Made me jump, there.'

'Why do I have to knock? This room is not off limits now,' she said. Her eyes were automatically drawn to the magazine Cliff had dropped on the floor. It was heavily illustrated and, at first, she couldn't make out what those shapes were, and then, somewhat embarrassed she looked up and met Cliff's shamefaced gaze.

'Aye, well, you've caught me out. Sorry about that, but if you'd knocked...'

She picked it up and closed it. The front bore the legend: 'Women how you like them – the bigger the better. Size 38DD and beyond!!!'

Cliff cleared his throat. 'I was looking for something and ... and the magazines were here, and I just found myself caught up with them for a moment.'

Looking around, Natalia observed that the place was in some disarray, which wasn't like Cliff.

Natalia shook her head. 'So this is where 1000/A2 has got to. This is what I've been sent to find.' She placed the magazine on top of a teetering pile, next to which stood another pile.

'What, you mean they sent you to fetch these naughty mags? You'll never carry them out for a start, they're too heavy.'

'You won't mind helping me then.'

'They've been claimed already?' Cliff asked, sounding disappointed, looking at the magazines longingly. 'I heard a taxi driver handed them in. He was going to take them for recycling, but changed his mind, seeing they're quite a collection dating back to the 1950s. Hoping for a reward, no doubt.'

'Quite a collection indeed,' Natalia agreed drily.

'Och, well.' Cliff rubbed his hand over his bristly grey hair. 'Where do you want them?'

'In fact, we don't need to move them today. As long as they're ready for pickup tomorrow.'

'I'll make sure of that, lassie,' Cliff said. 'I just stumbled on them by accident like when I was looking for something else.'

'That something else wouldn't be this, would it?' Natalia bent to retrieve an item she saw lying right beside Cliff's camping stool. It was Avon's missing hooter.

'Aye, that's the very thing. I've been hunting high and low for it. You do believe me, lassie?' Cliff took it out of her hand and started to tweak the rubber bulb, but Natalia put out a hand to stop him. One blast and Avon would come running in.

'I do, Cliff. I do.'

'She was that upset I thought I'd look for it in the vault. And I came across it just now in that cardboard box of, er, appliances.' He gestured to a box containing vibrators. 'And then I spotted the magazines and thought I'd have a wee break.'

'It was in here?'

'That's right. I'm in and out of here every day and not seen it before. It's not the sort of place you'd think of looking for it, is it?

134

These boxes were under the shelving here, and must've been disturbed when the magazines were brought in. I've no idea who's been sending those emails, though. Avon's really in a state over them.'

Avon. Natalia looked at Cliff thoughtfully. Judging from the rapt attention he'd been paying the magazine, a magazine devoted to the fleshy charms of the 'larger lady', Avon would have just the sort of voluptuous figure that would appeal to Cliff. She remembered how he often seemed snarly around Avon. On those few occasions when he'd clumsily offered help or sympathy she had pushed him away, both physically and emotionally. It was as if she did not want to be near him. But Cliff wasn't bad looking for his age, if he let his dour expression break into a twinkle. What could Avon have against him, apart from the fact that he wasn't Stefan?

'What is it?' he demanded. 'Why're you staring at me like that? I didn't take her hooter, you know.'

'I'm sure you didn't.' Natalia was beginning to form her suspicions about who that could be. 'I expect you'll be returning it to Avon soon. You know, she is very sensitive to smells.' Natalia pulled at his sleeve and sniffed. 'You smoke a sweet briar tobacco and it reminds me of my great uncle Jan, who smokes a similar brand. I like it, but maybe other ladies do not.'

Cliff shifted uncomfortably. 'I think I understand you,' he said. 'You think I should try and give it up.'

'Have you thought about it? Sporty man like you, bad for the lungs.'

'I've smoked since I was a wee lad. We all did in those days, on the back streets of the East End of Glasgow.' He drew in a rasping breath. 'Mebbe you're right. Mebbe it's time to stop.'

'OK. But promise me – don't give Avon the hooter till tomorrow. One more quiet day, please?' Natalia glanced at her watch. 'I must go, I'm meeting Rasheda, and then we're heading to Mornington Crescent.'

'Mornington Crescent! You win then,' Cliff said, a sudden gaiety in his voice.

'Win? Why do people act so strangely when I talk about that station?'

'You don't know the game then.'

'No. Is there a game called Mornington Crescent?'

'There is, and very funny, too.'

'Will you explain the rules to me?'

Cliff gave a rasping laugh. 'Oh aye, the

rules. It's like this, the contestants have to name London Underground stations – it has to be in a certain sequence, you know, and then at the right moment, someone says "Mornington Crescent" and they've won!'

'Let me see,' Natalia said, frowning. 'You win by naming that station? But why? And why are you still laughing?'

'Aye, well, the rules are very complex – too complex to go into right now. As soon as I figure them out myself, I'll let you know. You'll have to listen to it yourself, then you'll get the gist. Did I mention that the show is a comedy programme?'

'Ah.' Natalia smiled. British humour. She thought she was getting the hang of it, and then the next moment she came across something even more bizarre.

'I'll store it in here till tomorrow.' Cliff said, holding up the hooter and dropping it back in a small box of vibrators.

At home, later that night, Dermot silently passed the handset to Natalia. The gesture was nonchalant – he barely met her eyes. She scrambled to her feet, and went towards the door, stuffing a finger in her ear to block out the sounds of the football on TV.

'You have news for me, Harika?' she

asked, trying not to let her breathing betray her excitement.

'I may have something,' said Harika.

Natalia had to put her hand on the edge of the sink as her legs suddenly felt weak. 'Yes?'

'You mentioned that Jem's parents left Turkey for Cyprus in 1978, and then came to England in 1994.'

'You've found them?'

'Quite possibly,' said Harika. 'You said their surname was Aybar?'

'That's right,' said Natalia. Jem's parents had disapproved of his choice of bride from the start. They didn't attend the wedding, nor did they show any interest when Paul was born. Eventually, Jem had stopped bothering with them altogether. At times, Natalia wondered whether he'd have turned out the way he did if his family had remained tight-knit like her own.

'There are hundreds of Aybars in London,' said Harika, 'but a woman by the name of Saadet Aybar died last week.'

'That's Jem's mother.'

'It might be,' said Harika. Natalia always thought Harika would stay calm, even if she won the lottery. 'There was a death notice in *Toplum Postasi* – the Turkish newspaper printed in London.'

'And what about Kambil?' asked Natalia, with a sinking feeling. Even when she had first met Jem, his father's health had been failing. Surely there was no chance he was still alive.

'Kambil put the notice into the paper,' said Harika. 'His address is just off the Kingsland Road.'

Natalia could hardly get out her words. 'Do you have it?'

'Mrs O'Shea,' said Harika, in a serious tone. 'I'm happy to give you the address, as it's public knowledge. But I'd counsel you to think hard before contacting Mr Aybar. Ask yourself if this will bring you peace, or make things more difficult.'

More difficult? Perhaps Harika was more observant than Natalia had given her credit for. Perhaps she saw through Natalia's attempts to hide her emotions on the occasions they'd met.

'I will,' said Natalia. Her eyes were drawn to Paul's picture on the fridge. 'I have a pen here. What's the address?'

She wrote as Harika dictated. Kambil Aybar lived on Nuttall Street. It was literally fifteen minutes walk from their house. As she finished writing, Natalia realised that her hand was shaking.

'Thank you, Harika,' she said. 'For every-thing.'

'It's my pleasure, Natalia. Have a good evening.'

She hung up, and Natalia took a few deep breaths. Her mind travelled down the streets away from her house, turning imaginary corners along the route to Nuttall Street. She envisaged walking up the front steps of number seventeen, knocking on her father-in-law's door...

Wait, Natalia, she warned herself. Don't get carried away. He might not even want to see you.

She folded the paper, pocketed it, and walked back into the lounge, where Dermot hadn't moved.

'Everything OK?' he asked, but his atten-tion was firmly focused on the television.

Natalia thought about telling him what Harika had said, but a niggling feeling told her not to. Dermot was patient about her search, but she didn't want him to think her priorities lay elsewhere.

'No news,' she said. 'Just a boring ques-tion.'

If Dermot could see she was lying, he didn't let on.

12

Nuttall Street would have been quite grand one hundred and twenty years before, when it was built for the sprawling merchant classes of Victorian London. Now, number seventeen was just as run down as the other houses in the terrace. The pale-yellow paint was flaking off the wide bay window at the front, and the curtains drawn across at half-past four in the afternoon were grubby. Weeds sprouted defiantly between the flags in the small front yard. At some point in the past, someone, probably local youths with too much time on their hands, had lit a fire in the plastic recycling bin. One side was crusted and sagged where it had melted and reset.

Natalia had already walked the street twice, going over her first words, steeling her nerves. Donna had let her leave the Baker Street office early on account of a doctor's appointment. Natalia hated lying under almost any circumstances, but where the subject of her missing son was concerned, she found she could do so with only a small prick of guilt.

It was on her third pass that the front door opened. Natalia was caught in a moment of indecision: stop and engage; or walk on innocently. But it wasn't the face of Kambil Aybar that emerged from the door. A young woman, perhaps twenty-two, was manhandling a racing bike through the narrow entrance. From her dark features, and slightly oriental eyes, Natalia guessed she was from Malaysia or the Philippines. When the woman saw her, she smiled briefly. Natalia smiled back, feeling foolish.

'Is everything all right?' said the woman.

This was her chance. Natalia nodded. 'Yes, I'm sorry, but do you live here?'

The woman closed the door behind her, and looked back at the house. 'Yes,' she said. 'I've lived upstairs for six months.'

Natalia noticed that there were two buzzers by the front door. Of course, the single house, like so many others in London, was split into flats. She decided to get straight to the point.

'I'm looking for Kambil Aybar,' she said. 'Does he live here as well?'

The young woman had wheeled her bike

down the front steps and came alongside Natalia.

'There's a man living downstairs,' she said, lowering her voice. 'He's Turkish, I think, but we've never been introduced. Quite elderly.'

'Thank you,' said Natalia.

The girl swung a leg over her saddle and cycled off towards Kingsland Road. Natalia watched her go, then climbed the four front steps to the porch. She rang the lower bell. Behind transparent plastic, she could make out the faded letters of her former father-in-law's name. There was no doubt Harika's information was correct.

She tried to keep her breathing calm, but her heart was thumping. The last time she'd seen Kambil had been at a painful dinner, when Jem's parents had visited them in Poland before they were married. She'd gone to bed and heard father and son arguing downstairs. At the time, her Turkish was almost non-existent, and she'd been glad of it. The cause of their argument was clear enough though, and Jem had told her later that his parents were traditional and con-servative and wanted him to return to Turkey. The unspoken implication was that Natalia would not be welcome. The next morning, Kambil and Saadet had left before breakfast.

Now it wasn't so much fear at meeting Kambil again that made her palms sweat. She was a different person; braver, more sure of herself. No, the anxiety that twisted in her belly was that all this could come to nothing. She had daydreamed countless times in the preceding days the route here from the office, imagined the conversation with her former father-in-law and its wealth of possibilities. In her mind, it was a road opening up that led to one destination: Paul.

No one came to the door, and she could see nothing through the frosted-glass panels. Natalia felt disappointment begin to settle on her like a heavy cloud. She rang again anyway and waited.

This time, a dark shape appeared at the end of the hallway inside. The person moved slowly, with a noticeable limp on his left leg. Natalia practised her facial expression, hoisting and lowering her smile to find one suitable for the occasion. As the figure reached the door, and stood just a couple of feet away on the other side, she suddenly panicked that he might not recognise her at all. It had been over ten years.

She heard the latch click, and the door opened. It took a second or two to register, but there was no doubt the man in front of her was Kambil. He had become a very old man. Natalia remembered him being taller than her ex-husband – at least six foot two – but perhaps that was something to do with his haughtiness and bearing. Now he was only a fraction taller than Natalia herself, with hunched shoulders. He leaned heavily on a gnarled, wooden stick, and beneath his baggy trousers, shirt and cardigan, she could see his limbs were thin. His skin, which had once been dark, was the colour of washed-out ash. Natalia realised that the main impediment to recognising him was the fact that he'd shaved his once-bushy beard. Now a sprinkling of short, silver hairs bristled around his jaw. The hair on his head was a darker grey, thick and wavy around his fringe and ears.

'Hello, Natalia,' he said. His tone caught her off-guard. Kambil spoke as though they'd seen each other only the week before. There wasn't a jot of surprise beneath the bored formality. She was surprised that it angered her.

'Hello, Kambil,' she said. 'Can I come in?'

'I don't see why not,' he said, standing aside for her. His English had no trace of the East End, and he stressed each consonant ponderously.

Natalia slipped inside the door, and into the musty hallway. The blue carpet was threadbare in the centre, becoming thicker towards the edges. It was clean though, and Natalia guessed that Saadet had been the one responsible for regular vacuuming.

'I read about your wife,' said Natalia. 'I'm sorry for your loss.'

Kambil was still facing the door and closed it silently. When he turned to face her, his dark eyes met hers briefly, then dropped. 'She was a good woman. A good wife.'

He walked past her, and towards a door opposite the bottom of the stairs. Natalia supposed she was to follow, even though Kambil offered no invitation. He pushed open the door to his flat and she went inside after him. She found herself in a living room, with a dining table set at the rear. A couch and a tall-backed armchair were arranged near the bay window and focused on a small, ancient television with an old-fashioned aerial perched on top. Through a door at the rear, Natalia could see a freestanding electric oven, and there was another closed door that she guessed lead to a bedroom. The flat was tiny.

'Can I get you a drink?' Kambil asked her. 'Some coffee perhaps?'

This is surreal, Natalia thought. It's as though the past never happened. Still, there was something of a command in his request, so Natalia thought it best to go along at his pace.

'That would be lovely, thank you.'

Kambil shuffled into the kitchen. She wondered if he needed time to think. She certainly did. She had half-expected him to slam the door in her face, or at least express some force of emotion.

Her eyes were drawn to a bookshelf beside the armchair, where several framed photographs were standing. There was one of Saadet with a very elderly woman, who Natalia guessed was her mother. There was another of Kambil and Saadet in black and white on their wedding day, beaming under a stone-arched doorway. Fatima was pictured, too, holding a baby. And there was Hamesh, wearing his mortar board and holding the rolled script that announced his graduation from the University of Ankara. There wasn't a single picture of Jem, or Paul.

Kambil came into the room holding a tray with a long-spouted silver coffeepot, and two small cups. Alongside were two glasses of iced water. He sighed as he bent down to place it on the table. 'Take a seat,' he said.

Natalia did as he instructed, sitting on the edge of the armchair while Kambil eased himself onto the couch. He poured the coffee into the cups and sat back.

'I don't know where he is.'

The words were spoken without sadness, without any hint of feeling, and Natalia didn't know how to react. Did he mean Paul or Jem?

'I've been looking for him for a long time,' said Natalia.

'Jemal was always a headstrong boy,' said Kambil. 'He left home for the first time when he was six, after a minor beating.' He smiled, showing sparkling white teeth that had to be false. 'A friend found him walking the streets half a mile from our house with a bag containing a loaf of bread and a water bottle. When my friend asked Jemal where he was going, he told him "I'm going to make my father sorry".'

Kambil looked sadly at Natalia for a second, then reached forward and took his coffee cup. 'Of course, his mother spoilt him for days after that, and all was forgotten. She never understood the purpose of discipline.'

Natalia, to give her hands something to do, picked up her cup and blew on the black coffee. 'Have you heard from him? From Jem, I mean.'

Kambil lifted his head, in what might have been mistaken for a nod if she hadn't known the custom of his people. It implied a negative. 'He was right, I suppose,' said Kambil wistfully. 'He did make his father sorry.'

They drank their coffee in silence for a minute or more.

'Fatima is in touch with her brother still, and Hamesh every so often. He sent letters to his mother, but I never read them.'

Natalia felt her frustration grow hot in her chest. *You silly man,* she thought. *Behaving like a child.* She had not wanted to confront him, but leaving things unsaid was unhealthy.

'Weren't you even interested in how he was doing?' she asked. 'How your grandson was growing up?'

Suddenly, the old fire was in Kambil's eyes, and Natalia was back in the living room of their house in Poland and remembering that first time he fixed her with his gaze, but it died as quickly as it flared.

'I have no grandson,' he said through his teeth. 'I have no son.'

Why had she let herself hope at all? This was useless. Jem's father hadn't changed one bit. He was the same prejudiced brute even in his eighth decade.

'I know that you never welcomed my marriage to your son. It hurt me a great deal, because I loved him so much back then. But it hurt him far more. I'm not here to look for your forgiveness, or for your approval, I'm here because I think you might be able to help me find my boy, Mr Aybar. You lost your son through your own choices, mine was taken from me. I don't expect that you will want to help me, but there is no reason why you shouldn't. I've never purposefully done you any harm.'

She took a breath, and studied Kambil. His eyes were fixed on the photos beside her. It wasn't clear if he was staring at his wife, or his children, or even the empty space where Jem should have been. Where she might once have been, too.

'I think you should leave,' he said. 'I can't help you.'

So that was it. After an absence of ten years, they had covered all the ground they needed to in less than ten minutes. She felt like shouting at him, but also strangely drained.

Natalia's training took over. She had dealt with situations like this before, in her old job at the adoption agency back in Poland.

Countless times, over similar tables, in similar nondescript houses, she had acted as mediator to fractured families coming together again. She knew when it was time to leave.

This man had spent his life in charge of people. His business, his wife, his children. He had watched as his circle of influence had dwindled to nothing but a small flat in Hackney. Any shred of contempt in her was overshadowed by pity.

Natalia stood up, and reached into a bag for a slip of paper with her address written on it.

'Thank you for the coffee,' she said, her voice a little croaky. 'I'm very sorry about Mrs Aybar.' She placed the paper beside the tray. 'Please remember, I still have a son.'

Kambil sat as still as a statue in his seat, and she left him there, letting herself out of the front door. Only when she was back out on the Kingsland Road did she take a tissue out of her handbag and wipe her eyes. Whether for the sad old man or for herself, she wasn't sure.

13

Stood on the concourse of St Pancras International Station, Rasheda by her side, Natalia followed the approach of a petite woman heading directly for them, weaving through the Saturday crowds. The woman drew close. Thin and wiry, her tightly curled hair was cut short to her head showing off her shapely skull.

'Rasheda, so good to see you. Babe, you look amazing. How long has it been?'

Rasheda was wearing black, linen trousers that fell straight legged from her generous hips, and a scoop-necked, white T-shirt pinched in at the waist by a wide, white belt decorated in gold studs and a beaded necklace. Her freshly braided hair was held in place by a gold headband.

'Too long, Najjah, too long. You still skinny as always. You want to get some meat on those bones. I'm frightened I'm going to crush you!'

The two old friends embraced, laughing, looking each other up and down.

'You feel those muscles. I'm strong, just as I always was.'

Najjah's large eyes shone softly behind rimless spectacles.

'It's true,' Rasheda said to Natalia. 'She work harder than anyone else. This my friend Natalia – Natalia, Najjah.'

Natalia smiled. 'Hi, Najjah, good to meet you.'

'See what doing one good turn for a friend has done, helped find an old one,' Rasheda said. 'Najjah and me trained together five years ago.'

'You bet. Me and Rasheda very highly trained executives, cleaning class.' They giggled together. 'Those boys of yours been keeping you too busy to see old friends?'

'And some. Jason's a policeman now, London Transport division. Daniel, well, he's taking his exams, whether he wants to or not. How 'bout your family?'

The three women talked as they walked through the concourse. Either side, mellow London brick had been preserved for the walls, soaring up to the old, arching decorative-glass ceiling, high above the Eurostar trains and champagne bar on the next level. An escalator led from the concourse to the upper level and the platforms. Natalia took one last lingering look at the long-distance trains to Paris and beyond. Escape, flight from responsibility, was not an option. She felt a sudden yearning for Europe, for other old cities, for her homeland of Poland. She could just jump on a train and go!

'They fine. Another new grandchild, a little girl.' She sighed. 'I wish Thomas was still here to see her.'

Discovering that her old friend worked the Mornington Crescent area, Rasheda had told Natalia that Najjah had been widowed ten years ago when her husband was killed crossing a road, by a drunk driver. She'd brought up four children, all now flown the nest.

'Thank you for coming in,' Natalia said to her now. 'Don't you normally sleep all day after your night shift?'

'Bless you,' Najjah said. 'I work four nights on. I come home six o'clock, sleep till twelve, then I have a little zizz in the evening. And last night was one of my nights off anyway.'

They had to negotiate two flights of stairs and the usual ticket barriers down to the Northern Line platform for Camden Town, to change there for Mornington Crescent.

'Do you always work at Mornington Crescent?'

'That's been my station for the past year. I expect I'll be rotated on soon. The bosses don't want us getting too comfortable anywhere.'

'Oh no!' Rasheda nodded, laughing with her.

'You know the station very well now, then.'

'I do. It's over a hundred years old. We got many old features. I like to keep it nice.'

'How big is your team?'

'Usually about five of us. We go in our own entrance, and clean the service rooms and offices first. We start upstairs, then come to ground level, and then have our break 'bout midnight, half past. Hot drink, sandwich, chocolate biscuits – we get the munchies in the middle of the night. After that, we come out into the public areas where the passengers go.'

Reaching Camden Town, they descended the few steps to their platform.

'How are you coping with the electricity being turned off at night at the moment?' Natalia asked.

'We bring a thermos flask. They rig up emergency lighting for us. It strange though, sort of blue light. You don't see the dirt so good.'

'Where are the electricians working?'

'Oh, they way down the tunnel. They go in about eleven and we don't see them till they come up at five and we all go home. Here we are!'

All three stood up, Rasheda fanning herself against the heat in the carriage, and descended onto the platform. A handful of other passengers got off at the same time. The doors slid shut and the train rattled on its way, gathering speed as it disappeared into the arched tunnel.

Once the train and the passengers had gone, Natalia listened. It was quiet, the lighting dim. The walls were lined with small cream tiles, with a dark-blue motif running along above waist height. At one end of the platform was a big, brown wooden door marked 'Private'. At regular intervals were old, wooden, backless benches to sit on, punctuated by big, circular, white-plastic discs on the wall, with two buttons to press; blue for information and green for emergency situated below a red fire alarm. One of the newer safety features that Jonathan Crane must have been referring to.

'See?' Najjah said. 'Lovely old place.'

'I wouldn't know where to start cleaning a station like this.' Rasheda said.

'We got our routine. 'Course, you need a

bigger brain to clean a station than an office!' She dug Rasheda in the ribs with her elbow.

'Cheek!'

'What about down there?' Natalia pointed to the rails themselves, heading deep into the tunnels.

'Ah, that's a special team. The "fluffers". They come through every week, picking out all the dust and whatnot that fall under the rails. They a very special group of people. Miles and miles of track to clean.'

'Being nibbled by the rats and mice all the way,' Rasheda shuddered.

'Can you show me where you've been finding the lost items?' Natalia asked.

'Sure. We can't go in there now, because it's locked, but I can point to it. That another reason I said to come by train, because it down here, not up above.'

As a young couple strolled on to the platform, arms round each other's waists, she led them to one of the cross routes between the northbound and southbound platforms. It was only a few yards long, but set into one side of it was a big, metal door with a small window in it, and black-and-yellow tape along one edge. It was marked 'Fire Exit'.

'There,' she pointed through the window.

157

'It was just up there.'

Natalia peered through, with Rasheda looking over her shoulder. She saw a few stairs leading upwards, with a handrail, a small landing, more steps, then no more.

'That Horace's area for cleaning.'

'Horace?'

'One of my team.'

'He comes down there and has the key to open that door, then relock it and come on to the platforms and join the others.' Najjah nodded seriously. 'Each thing he found was somewhere along that passageway and steps. Not easy to see, in the funny blue light, but he is very thorough.'

'Can we speak to Horace?'

'Horace don't speak to no one. He keep to himself. He a hard worker and I respects that.'

'Did he notice anything else? Anything unusual? Don't you think it odd that all those items found belong to women.'

'What's strange for me is how they get in there. Access at the top is through the station offices and staff are there all the day.'

'They come in at night?'

'But we are here. We would hear. We would see!' Najjah cried.

'This man is very clever. He has inside

knowledge of the system. From what you say, I think he must somehow bring the women in when you are all upstairs – because the CCTV is switched off at this station, due to the electrical maintenance going on, at ten o'clock. He must leave before you have your break. The question is, do they come willingly? Or is something more sinister happening?'

The three women paused, taking in what that could possibly mean, each shuddering in turn.

'But I must tell the others. We will look for him every night!'

Rasheda put her arms round Najjah. 'Don't worry, honey. Natalia will get to the bottom of this.'

'You have been incredibly helpful, finding those objects and handing them in,' Natalia told her. 'Without you, I would not have known about this.'

Najjah looked relieved. 'I want to go upstairs now, meet a friend of mine who works in the ticket office. We'll have lunch in the Hope and Anchor. You welcome to join us.'

'No, no, Najjah, I got a date with Primark, and then I got to be heading to work.'

'Thank you, Najjah,' Natalia added, 'for your time and help.'

After Najjah went, Rasheda and Natalia sat side by side on one of the benches, sharing a bottle of water while they waited for a train.

'So was that really helpful?' Rasheda asked.

'There are more questions than answers at the moment,' Natalia told her. 'But seeing where the woman lost their items, yes, that's made a big difference. One more piece of the puzzle to put into place. I'm sure I am right, but the police don't think there's anything to investigate.'

'Anything else I can do, let me know.'

'There is one thing – Jason. Could you ask him to let me know if he comes across any mention of a woman being assaulted in this area?'

'Sure, I'll ask him to keep his eyes and ears open.'

'Thanks. Now what's happening about Raymond?'

'Don't ask! I still can't decide what to do for the best. He texted me yesterday. Expectin' to be staying at my place when he comes out. It makes me so angry. It's not me he wants, it's just convenience. He needs to give a fixed address, terms of his release. Grrr. I feel so used. I told him no, but he just ignores me and what I want.'

'When is the release date?'

'It's been put back a few days, thank goodness. Something about the paperwork and signatures. But now he's saying he's going to call Daniel and arrange to take him out.'

'Daniel doesn't know yet?'

'No. I haven't found the right way to tell him his father is coming out, but he's not staying with us. When he hears,' she shook her head, 'I don't know how I'm gonna explain to him why his father is not with us. But what are the rules with something like this?'

Sitting back against the wall, both lost in their thoughts, Natalia's mind swam with all the possibilities. Polly couldn't remember being at Mornington Crescent station, and certainly not in a restricted area. Whoever took her there knew the CCTV was down, knew the cleaners took a tea break at midnight, and had access to slip a passenger into a restricted area. The question was, did they drag them there or did they go willingly? What happened to Polly Hansen and all these other women? If they were attacked, which was beginning to seem more and more likely, it could be anyone from one of the fluffers to the electricians to the cleaners, but how was Natalia going to prove any of it?

14

'Thank god it's–' Mark held up his hand.

'Friday!' Natalia slapped her hand to his. 'What are your plans for the weekend?'

'Dunno. Mate of mine wants me to give kayaking a go with him. I'm thinking about it.'

'At least it'll be cool on the water,' Natalia said, fanning herself, while, at the same time, glimpsing up towards one of the meeting room doors on the upper level.

Donna was in an early-morning breakfast conference with the Area Commander, no less. Perhaps there would be a chance to speak with him, on his way out. How many meetings did that make it this month? Natalia tried to count them up, but lost track. Donna seemed to have been out of the office attending liaison meetings with the Met every day – even several times a day. But this was the first time in a week Jonathan Crane had come to the LPO. Armed with fresh information, she was keen to have words with him.

'Yeah,' Mark carried on talking, 'my mate's a bit crazy. Into all these adventure holidays and extreme sports, like white water rafting and potholing and paragliding. Whereas *some* people.' He nodded towards the office notice board. 'Like to take things a bit more gently.'

'What's that?' she said.

'Go and take a look. I've been waiting for you to see them.'

Obligingly, Natalia threaded her way through the desks, saying hello to Ranjiv on the way, who nodded knowingly when he saw where she was heading.

The notice board was fixed to the back of the dividers between the office and reception. As Natalia drew near, she could see a series of photos had been pinned up. Then, close up, she saw the detail and had to break into a grin.

All the carefully manipulated 'hooter cards' had been pinned up in a row. Here was 'Hooter meets a publican' and 'Hooter on a scooter' outside Harrods next to one she hadn't seen before. She stepped closer and carefully studied 'Hooter catches a bus', a photograph taken front on of a double decker bus, with Hooter at the doors. And who was that in 'Hooter makes a friend'?

163

The hooter was positioned beside a stunning-looking girl with long, blonde hair and a very skimpy dress, the photo taken in a bar. She was holding a cocktail and Hooter wore dark glasses.

Natalia headed back to Mark.

'They're a – hoot – aren't they?' he said.

'She obviously hasn't seen them yet.'

They looked over towards Donna's office. While Donna was in her meeting, Avon had positioned herself at Donna's desk for the afternoon.

'Mark, have you been involved with making them?' Natalia asked.

'Me? No way. Do you think Hooter would be seen with the likes of me? He's obviously got more sophisticated tastes.'

From the corner of her eye, Natalia saw Cliff emerging from the vault. He was glowering even more than usual. Stefan had told her he was on a very short fuse today, the slightest thing was setting him off.

What was eating him?

'When Avon sees, she'll go mad.'

'Postcards from her old friend Hooter? Surely not...'

Cliff was hovering near Avon's desk. Then, instead of continuing outside, as Natalia expected, he turned to go back to the vault.

But Avon had seen him. She was standing up behind Donna's desk and now came beetling over in full warrior mode.

'Cliff McDougal, just what were you doing?' She bore down on him, brown eyes blazing behind her spectacles, the fiery streaks in her hair aflame.

Cliff was stopped in his tracks. 'Nothing,' he growled.

'Nothing?' Avon pounced. 'Then exactly what is this doing on my desk?'

She held the hooter aloft over her head, brandishing it so that everyone could see.

'Please don't,' Mark groaned, stuffing his fingers in his ears. 'Cliff, I won't forgive you.'

Sure enough, Avon could not resist squeezing the bulb. The hooter let out a satisfyingly loud *toot toot*.

Natalia glimpsed the startled expression of a client in reception.

'What have you got to say for yourself?' Avon demanded. 'As if it wasn't bad enough stealing it, but sending all those postcards on my email. You've got a warped sense of humour, Cliff McDougall.'

Natalia's eyes flew to the postcards on the notice board. Don't look round, Avon, she prayed, or you'll go ballistic.

'I didna take yer damned hooter,' Cliff spluttered eventually. 'I found it. And I'm returnin' it to its rightful owner. But I'm thinkin' I'm wishin' I hadn'e now.'

'How convenient. You just found it. And where was it hiding all this time? Where you could take photos of it and pester me with them?'

Silently, Stefan had also come out from the vault. His dark-navy eyes observing the scene.

Natalia held her breath.

'Well, I'll thank you to keep your thieving hands off my desk.' Avon plonked the hooter down and stood with her hands on her hips, glaring at Cliff.

'I've never laid a hand on your desk, thieving or otherwise, till today.' Cliff squared up to her, his brows lowered and a fierce expression on his face.

Had Avon met her match? Perhaps this was what she needed, someone who would stand up to her. And, as the oldest-serving member of the office, Cliff had the standing and confidence that said he was her equal.

But Natalia knew she had to intervene now, before the slanging match escalated into all-out war. Stepping forward, she called, 'Stefan, is there anything you'd care to say?'

166

She had to do it.

'Me?' He laughed. 'How can you say that, Natalia?'

All heads swivelled towards her. Even Avon's mouth was closed for once.

'Because it was *you* who took the hooter, and who has been creating all the very clever postcards.'

There was a murmur of appreciation for Stefan's creativity, but he was still holding out on her.

'Your facts are wrong this time, Detective O'Shea. How can it be me?'

'Oh, but the evidence is overwhelming, and it's right over there.' Natalia pointed towards the notice board. 'Hooter catches a bus. It's on its way to Willesden Junction, passing through West Hampstead, where you live.'

Avon was glaring, outraged, at the row of postcards.

'Anyone can take a picture of a bus anywhere they like,' Stefan shrugged engagingly, but Natalia could see he was trying not to laugh. She had him.

'And Hooter's lovely friend in the bar? I remember her, she was at your thirtieth birthday party.'

'OK, OK, I admit it. It was me. Cliff, you spoiled the game.'

There was a ripple of applause for Stefan's inventiveness and audacity but then, show over, Natalia's colleagues turned back to their desks.

'I want a word with you, young man,' Cliff growled, and stamped off into the vault. 'I'll be waiting for you downstairs.'

Natalia saw the expression of mingled horror, fury and misery on Avon's face. For once, she had nothing to say, but sat down with her back to them all, nursing the hooter. Natalia beckoned Stefan over.

'I think I know why you did it,' she said softly, looking towards a large-brimmed, straw hat, hanging on a clotheshorse above Avon's desk. The very same straw hat that Natalia had spotted on the cctv cameras when she went to see Omar at Bank. 'Avon's been following you, my little brother.'

The expression of relief on Cliff's face was instantaneous. 'She's been stalking me,' he murmured back. 'I go to my local super-market, she is there. In my local pub, she is having a drink. In the morning, I look both ways. Will she be there, in the street? I want to shout at her, leave me alone, but I think she wants this, to speak with me. What do I do?'

In his agitation, Stefan's Serbian accent

had become stronger. Natalia laid a hand on her friend's arm, not caring if Avon saw. Let her think what she would. 'So you put the postcards up just now. You want to turn her against you?'

'I hope so. I was going to do it privately, not in front of everyone, but we had to save Cliff.'

Natalia nodded. 'Avon needs a man. She thinks it's you, we know it isn't. But there might be someone for her. Wait and see.'

'I hope he hurries up soon,' Stefan said. 'It's been really getting to me. But I must go now. Cliff is not happy with me.'

Natalia hovered at her desk, deliberating over something. That must have been what Stefan meant the other night when he said he had two problems, and that he thought he had one of them under control. But what could the other problem be? Avon's romantic fixation might explain Stefan's recent moodiness. Hopefully now he would return to his normal sunny self.

Bracing herself, she walked over to Donna's office, where Avon had retreated to.

'Avon, can I get you a cup of water? I was heading to the machine anyway.'

The poor woman looked miserable.

'Why would he do it? Why would he be so mean?' she moaned, holding her head in her hands.

The sound of a door opening made Natalia look up. Through the door from the stairs and lifts leading to the upstairs conference rooms came Donna, followed by Jonathan Crane. Judging by her glowing expression, it had been a successful meeting. The department boss had let her straight, blonde hair loose over her shoulders, though she still wore her severe, black trouser suit and fresh, white shirt.

Not wanting to abandon Avon now, Natalia took a seat opposite her colleague, her voice soft.

'Avon, we do not always choose who we have affection for, or who has affection for us. But love is not something that can be forced. We must be gentle with the ones who do like us though. Stefan was wrong to do what he did. But no one is blameless, are they?'

Natalia stared through the glass partition at Cliff. Avon followed her gaze, and a look of understanding passed between her and Natalia.

Above, the door from upstairs opened again and this time it was Jason who came through. He wore his British Transport

Police uniform and he had a serious look on his face. He must have been at the meeting, too, but Donna and Jonathan, deep in conversation, were strolling towards the exit as if they'd forgotten him.

Seeing Donna, Avon hurriedly gathered up her things, the moment between her and Natalia seemingly evaporated.

'Hadn't you best be getting back to work? I think we've all wasted enough time today.'

Taking her cue, Natalia hurried towards the exit, anxious not to miss this opportunity to speak with the Area Commander, only to be intercepted by Jason.

'Listen, Natalia.' He looked both ways and then lowered his voice. 'That thing you asked my mum for me to look out for. I think I've got some information for you.'

Natalia's heart quickened, and she led him to the side of the room, where they could not be heard.

15

'What's happened?' she asked.

'Yesterday it was, first thing in the morning, at the station – you know I'm at Camden Town still.'

Natalia nodded, feeling a sense of foreboding.

'Woman comes in, terrible state she was. Pretty badly beaten. But distressed. She was sobbing. And sort of disoriented. Said she'd been attacked, but didn't know where or by whom.'

'Oh no, it's happened again,' Natalia said softly.

'Yeah, well, I mean, it happens, but this was more like you were saying – a young woman, maybe about thirty, and it's weird because she can't remember anything about it.'

'So what did you do?'

'She was examined by the police doctor, and he found she had been sexually assaulted. He's taken some blood tests. We have his preliminary report, and now we have to wait for confirmation from the labs. But he's pretty sure.'

'Rohypnol?'

'Exactly. But how did you know?'

'I've been thinking. It's the only way these women could have been attacked and not remember anything about it.' Natalia thought of Polly and her feeling of helpless shame. Had Polly also been raped, but been too shamed to say? 'I was losing confidence in my fears. But perhaps now someone will take me seriously.'

'I'm sorry, Natalia, it's just a one-off as far as we're concerned. Sometimes these Rohypnol attacks are done by men known to the women.'

'How can they abuse someone who is helpless and unconscious?' Natalia was indignant.

'I know, I know. I don't like it any more than you do. If I think of someone doing that to Honey... But we can only bring a case when there are hard facts, forensics, or the CPS will throw it out. When the doctor's report is confirmed, I'll let you know, OK?'

'But what are the police going to do about it? What are your lines of enquiry?'

Jason looked uncomfortable. 'We don't really have any. She doesn't know when or where it happened, just some time on Wednesday night. She woke up in the porch of the house where she lives in the top-floor flat.'

'You have evidence there. Polly too woke up in the hallway of her own house.'

'Or it could just mean the woman managed to make it home while still under the influence of the drug, and then collapsed. And your Polly didn't file a report, did she?'

'But there must have been other incidents, I am sure of it. Some other woman must have come forward to the police. Surely a crosscheck could be made.'

Jason shrugged helplessly.

In the back of Natalia's mind was the awful thought that it seemed the sex attacker was beginning to escalate his activity. An increase in the level of violence used. Would a young woman's life have to be at stake before the police took action?

'Please, Jason, listen to me. I have all the evidence you need. I have a list of items found in Mornington Crescent station, all of them belonging to women, from jewellery to make-up to underwear. All found in a restricted area, or nearby, by the cleaning staff after the weekend. Let me give you the files I've printed off.'

Jason looked even more uncertain and more his young age. 'I'm really sorry, Natalia, you can give me the files, but I can just hear what Jack will say. That's no evidence at all. It's just a list of lost objects, end of. Not even circumstantial.'

'Are you ready, Constable?'

Jonathan Crane's voice came from behind her. As Jason straightened up and said, 'Yessir,' Natalia met the Area Commander's direct gaze, which was cool and assessing, as it travelled down her body. His tan had deepened, and his good looks combined with his quick intelligence must prove an irresistible combination to Donna, she could see.

'Commander Crane,' she said, aware that Jason was looking from one to the other of them with dismay. 'These attacks on young women. I have some more information for you. I've been to Mornington Crescent station now and—'

'Not now, Natalia,' Donna cut in, as Jonathan's eyebrows were lifting quizzically. 'We have to get a move on. This way, Jonathan.' She extended a hand to shepherd him away possessively.

'I just wanted to pass some information on.'

'We really do not have time for this.'

Donna's tone was as testy as Natalia had ever heard it. She turned to Jonathan and flashed him a winning smile. 'Natalia has an enquiring mind, something we encourage in our staff here. But it's too easy to start to read stories into the lost items we receive. I've only been here a short while, but I've learned a great deal from our experienced staff. Looking at so many objects every day, it's only human to start making connections. And that's just what this is, I'm sure, Natalia. Please stop worrying unnecessarily. Now, listen up, everyone,' Donna said, getting everyone's attention. 'I have an announcement to make.'

Donna succeeded in steering the Area Commander away from Natalia and over to the reception area. Jason threw Natalia an apologetic look, then followed.

Natalia stared after them, gritting her teeth in frustration. Trust Donna to be so dismissive. She always had her eye fixed firmly on the bigger picture, especially when it involved advancing her own career. Natalia was convinced Donna Harris would not want any minor inconvenience like one of her staff badgering a senior British Transport policeman to stand in her way.

'I've volunteered us for a simulation

exercise. It's being run by the British Transport Police, of course,' she said. 'They are the co-ordinating body. It's going to span two days, and all you have to do is be volunteer bodies for the emergency services to practise their skills on. So that when a real emergency arises, the training they will have received will immediately kick in, and lives will be saved.'

So that's what all the meetings had been about last week. She should have known Donna would have a special agenda.

16

Dermot's turn to prepare their supper, and he'd gone to some effort to buy asparagus and strawberries and some of their favourite Rocombe Farm organic ice cream. Standing side by side in the kitchen, she pared down the asparagus stalks, while he hulled the strawberries, and gently pan-fried the salmon

'Pour us some beer, love,' he said. 'I've got a terrible thirst on me, and my fingers are all sticky.'

Natalia fetched an ice-cold bottle from the fridge and poured it for him. 'It must be terrible working out at the site in all this heat,' she said. 'There's no shade at all.'

'Ah, I'm used to working in all weathers,' Dermot replied.

She looked at the line where his skin, a dark brown, turned milky white under his shirt. 'You'll have to take your shirt off,' she teased. 'Turn that lovely brown all over.'

She'd meant it as a compliment to his tan. And normally he'd have taken this as a cue to tease her about her pale, Slavic skin, maybe pulled back her top and run his fingers over her body. Instead, he said, 'You don't like me the way I am?' in a strange tone of voice.

'Of course I do.' Natalia put her arms round him and nuzzled his neck, then kissed it before turning back to her task. 'Tough day?'

'And then some. We're getting the foundations dug now. Coming across all kinds of historical things, right back to the Roman times.'

'What sort of things?' Natalia asked, interested. She put the asparagus in a saucepan of simmering water, picked up her glass of chilled rosé wine and perched on top of the breakfast stool.

'Lots of broken pottery and tiles. Buckles and buttons. Sure, a whole shoe shop of pieces of shoe leather–' He stopped suddenly.

'Are the archaeologists coming down from the Museum of London?

Dermot shook his head. 'I think they've got enough artefacts. They come by every now and then to keep a tally, make sure nothing special has turned up.' He took a pull of his beer, staring down at the two bowls of strawberries. 'And there are the bones.'

'Bones?' Natalia looked at him, searching his face.

'Ah, they're mostly animals; cattle, pigs and sheep. From the butchers and slaughterhouses. I'll take these bowls in and lay the table, OK?' He kissed the top of her head, then left their narrow galley kitchen and went into the living room.

That was the first inkling Natalia had that something was bothering him. He would tell her when he was ready, she decided. She wouldn't pester him.

They sat at the table to one side of their white-painted living room. All the windows stood open to let a very faint breeze in, which was blowing from the large park opposite and stirred the oatmeal coloured curtains. Natalia could see that the grass in the park was already turning brown. Big chestnut trees with canopies of dark-green leaves cast shade. Families picnicked on the grass, young people fooled about on bikes and teenagers listened to music, while older people strolled or sat on the benches. Dermot had put on the Loose Ends CD to listen to while they ate.

'Donna had the Area Commander in again today,' Natalia told her husband. 'I tried to tell him everything I've discovered about Mornington Crescent, but she was determined to get him away from me.'

Dermot nodded. 'Do you think you're gettin' a bit too involved in this Mornington Crescent thing,' he said carefully. 'It's not the same as when you helped out Peter Bookman. You don't think this ... this is to fill up a space?'

Puzzled, Natalia shook her head. 'My life is already very full. No spaces. I thought you had more faith in me, Dermot O'Shea,' she said lightly. 'Don't forget what Jason told me today. These young women need a voice. They need to be helped.'

'I hear you. It's what you do – did – in Poland, I know. Helping children and parents find each other again. But these young women here – it's all hypothetical, isn't it? A girl called Polly gets so drunk she can't recall where she lost her gran's necklace, and Jason tells you about a case of date rape. I'm sorry, Natalia, I can see why the Area Commander can't see a case there.'

Natalia nodded. 'True, if you only look at those facts. But what about all the items found in the same place?'

'I don't know, but I do know you're getting caught up in it.' Wearily, Dermot put down his knife and fork. That's when he said, 'I think I'll go out for a bit of a walk. Clear my head, like.'

'But your strawberries...'

'I'll have them later. I won't be long.' He bent down and kissed her cheek, then quietly left the room. Natalia heard him pick up his keys from the bowl on the small table in the vestibule, then let himself out. She strained to hear his cheerful whistle, but only heard his descending steps.

Natalia looked down at her plate. A couple of mouthfuls left. She chewed and swallowed, but the flavour had left the food. She reviewed the evening, recalling every detail of their conversation. Was it something in particular she had said? Was it because she insisted there was a case to be heard, that women were being assaulted by a serial sex attacker. Perhaps Dermot felt he was being sidelined, that she was not paying enough attention to him. Yet that was not the Dermot she knew. He had enough interests of his own and was not that dependent and needy. Or was she only seeing his true colours now, as they relaxed into their marriage?

Uneasily, she stacked their plates and began carrying them through into the kitchen to fill the waiting and empty dishwasher. She felt she should give Dermot the benefit of the doubt. Something had already been eating at him before he arrived home, that seemed most likely. She hoped he would share it with her at some point.

As Natalia filled the dishwasher, she glanced, as always, at the kitchen notice board on which they pinned the latest pictures of the children. There was Nuala in costume and make-up at one of her class productions. Connor beamed from his picture, front tooth missing, Dad's arm around his shoulders, both in white judo kit.

Finally, saved till last, her own son, Paul. Squinting into a Turkish sun, football in hand. Grief squeezed her heart, making her breathless for a moment. Where are you my darling? she asked silently. So near – somewhere in the UK – and yet so far, his whereabouts a secret guarded jealously by Jem.

She and Dermot had decided, after Christmas, to tell Nuala and Connor about Natalia's kidnapped son, and to start including him in their family. Both children had been interested, and Nuala's behaviour towards her had altered. Never a child to take prisoners, she could have used the information to subtly wound her father's new wife. Instead, she decided to be grown-up about it, and asked now and then if there was any news. Connor had simply said, 'Great. It'll be better with three of us to play football. I hope he comes home soon.'

But the excitement and joy of discovering that Paul was nearer to her had now worn away. Fatima had not written for two months. Stalemate was reached again. She took a deep breath. I'll never give up, son, never give up till I'm able to see you again, hold you in my arms. She could only hope that Jem had not poisoned their son's mind against her.

Dishwasher humming, glasses washed, she carried a cup of tea into the living room and looked around disconsolately. It was hard to settle to anything. Natalia picked up the

Evening Standard and began to read of the daily problems that plagued Londoners. Traffic chaos, public transport chaos, impossible heat, plagues of rats and mice, hospital chaos. From the picture the newspaper painted, you'd almost expect to see corpses piled in the streets, she thought.

What was that?

It was faint, but she was sure she'd heard a terrible wail, coming from her neighbour's flat. She got to her feet. The walls in the modern, purpose-built block of flats were insulated and they rarely heard any sound. The young Sri Lankan couple had had their first baby three months ago. Occasionally, they heard the baby crying, but very faintly, through the wall. This was different.

A loud hammering sounded at her front door. She ran through and opened it.

'Please ... please ... baby ... come!' It was Sunil, the baby's father. His dark eyes were starting from his head, his expression distraught.

Without thinking, Natalia grabbed up her handbag from the vestibule table and ran after him, slamming the door shut behind her. Sunil was already inside his flat, the door standing open. She followed him inside.

Another terrible howl came from the bedroom. Please, God, let the baby be OK, she prayed.

The bedroom was painted white. A large, double bed stood in the middle, with folded coverlets of brown and white. There was a dressing table and stool. On one wall was a very large, framed tapestry depicting Eastern celestial beings, decorated in sequins and gold thread.

In one corner stood a cot. Beside it was Araminda. She wore a sari, and had pulled the scarf up over her face. She was making a terrible moaning, gasping sound, rocking to and fro. Sunil had positioned himself at the foot of the cot.

Natalia came up beside Araminda who turned to her and spoke in her own language. Natalia looked down, dreading what she might see. Was it a cot death?

The baby was alive. But the little boy's back was arching, his little arms and legs flailing. His head with its thatch of black hair was on one side, but Natalia could see his eyes were rolled up in his head under fluttering lids. He was having convulsions of some kind.

Something else took her over. 'Ambulance,' she said, taking out her mobile phone. 'Cold water,' she instructed Sunil, as she dialled 999. Her call was answered immediately and as she was talked through the necessary information she indicated to Araminda to gently stroke her baby's hand. She didn't know what to do. Her first-aid training, learned in Poland when she first started work, covered burns, scalding, cuts and bruises, minor sprains. How she wished now she'd gone further.

The calm, male operator told her to hang up. 'The paramedic will call you from the ambulance,' he said.

Within moments, as Sunil began sponging his baby's arms and legs with cool water, her mobile rang. 'I'm Sandra, the paramedic. We're on our way.'

Natalia could hear doors slamming, the gunning of an engine, and then the ambulance siren, as Sandra began asking for details of the baby's condition.

The next ten minutes were completely nerve-wracking, even as she relayed Sandra's instructions to the baby's distraught parents. Time seemed to stretch endlessly as the little baby would relax, come to, then be seized by another convulsion. How could its tiny body withstand whatever powerful forces had invaded it? Even though Natalia knew just how strong and many were the survival mechanisms of very small babies, she marvelled at how he withstood such rigours. Tears poured down his mother's face as she crooned to him, and his father carried out the instructions relayed by Natalia from the paramedic.

And then they were here. Sandra and Bill, the driver, both in greens. Sandra barely in her twenties, Bill in his forties, surrounding the cot with their emergency medical packs and equipment, efficiently taking over, administering oxygen, talking brightly and reassuringly to all present.

'We'll be taking him into hospital now,' Sandra said to Sunil and Araminda. 'You can come with us in the ambulance.'

'Come, too, please,' Sunil begged Natalia.

She looked at Sandra, who nodded.

Feeling limp with relief Natalia followed down the four flights of stairs as Sandra and Bill carried the baby in a specially adapted medical cot, Sunil and Araminda behind, Araminda still weeping from shock. All she could hope for was that they were in time and the baby's life saved. What came next, she could not imagine. It would all depend on what had caused the baby's seizures. She wouldn't think about that now.

Natalia and the baby's parents could only

watch as Sandra tended to the little boy and Bill wove the ambulance as fast and expertly as he could through the evening traffic to Homerton Hospital in Hackney.

Once there, after they had washed their hands with the disinfectant at the hospital entrance, she helped Sunil, whose English was patchy at the best of times, to go through the registration process, while Araminda followed the baby into ICU. Then she phoned home and left a message on the answering machine.

'Here,' Dermot handed her a plastic cup of coffee from the vending machine in the hospital corridor, then sat down beside her, holding his own cup of coffee between his hands. Natalia had been at the hospital for an hour now, where Dermot had come to find her.

'Thanks,' she said and gulped some of it gratefully, then laid her head momentarily on his shoulder. 'I suppose we should go home, now Sunil and Araminda have some relatives here.' Opposite them in the hospital corridor sat the young couple, dark circles round their eyes, with Sunil's brother and his wife, talking quietly together. 'We know the baby's crisis has passed.'

'Ah, we may as well wait a bit longer. See if there's any news. There's nothing on telly tonight anyway.' He succeeded in raising a smile from her. 'I must admit, I was a bit worried when I came in and found the flat empty,' he said. 'And then thank goodness I checked the answering machine.

'I was so glad you came,' she said.

Dermot drained his cup and said, 'Sorry about earlier. Something got to me today. The bones we uncovered. One was the skeleton of a child. Hundreds of years old. But it just ... I felt so sorry for the poor wee mite, all twisted up it was.'

Natalia took his hand. Life was so precious, and he was such a good father. If only she could–

'Mr and Mrs Bandranathar?' Mr Kitson, the head paediatrician, wearing blues, had come to join them. Sunil looked to Natalia and Dermot to join them.

'Our neighbours,' he told the consultant. 'Saved baby's life.'

Mr Kitson nodded. 'I'm pleased to tell you,' he said. 'That baby's convulsions have ceased and he's resting comfortably. His life signs are as optimum as we'd expect them to be at this stage. He's a real little fighter.'

There was a general murmur of joy as the

Bandranathar family embraced each other.

'But,' he continued, 'as yet we don't know the cause for the convulsions, nor the extent of any damage caused. It could be due to a very high temperature from a virus, made worse by the summer heat. It's possible that there are other explanations. We've taken tests. Now all we can do is wait for the results and then we will discuss them with you.'

Natalia and Dermot, no longer needed, said their goodbyes and slipped away, holding hands. Natalia could only squeeze helplessly back, realising how there was no rhyme or reason to any of this. She had thought that by staying true to her son's memory, she would in time be rewarded, but tragedy could strike at any moment, and blindside you.

And then, unbidden and unwanted, the picture flashed into her mind of little Paul in the kindergarten playground, his father looming over him saying, 'Come on, Paul, let's go.'

Had there been something in his father's manner that had alarmed him? Had he asked, 'Where's Mummy?' And when they were speeding away in the car and he realised that she wasn't there, what were his thoughts then? Had he called out for her, or had Jem reassured him that all would be well?

It seemed there were no rules in love or life.

17

Natalia opened her London A–Z street map again, and looked down at the slip of paper, tucked inside, with an address written on it. Exiting the 1930s, brick building at Golders Green tube, she referred to her map before crossing the busy junction of North End Road at the lights and heading north up along the Finchley Road. Passing the parade of shops, she eventually reached a row of old-style, brick mansion blocks on her right.

The spiral-bound book felt slippery in her hot hand. Lifting her sunglasses so that she could read more clearly, she checked the map again. Leaving her finger on the spot, she looked up. Yes, there was Blackbird Avenue opposite. This street was quiet and shady. Well-established sycamores and London planes were planted in the pavements on either side, their leaves limp in the early-evening heat. The roots had caused the pavement to rise up here and there, tripping up the unwary, but Natalia was glad for their cool shade.

She looked down again at the slip of paper on which she'd copied the address from the file at work. Number forty-four. Yes, here it was. Many of the other streets she'd passed had featured white, pebbledash houses, but this street was from an earlier period. The row of buildings was built in red brick, with white-painted, decorative stone facings around windows and at the apex of the roofs. One of the houses proclaimed a date of 1892. They were two storeys, but many of the roofs boasted Velux windows, showing that attic space had been converted to more living area. It seemed that Londoners everywhere were building upwards, outwards, even downwards into their basements, to create more room.

Like its neighbours, number forty-four had a porch supported by turned wooden posts. Natalia pushed through the peeling wooden gate, and went to the front door, heart speeding up in anticipation. Beside the front door were two bell pushes, each with a named pasted below it.

Polly Hansen lived in the ground-floor flat. Natalia pressed the bell and heard a loud ring somewhere inside. She'd phoned earlier, but there had been no reply. She wondered whether Polly would recognise her and allow her to come in.

She heard a door opening and the shuffle of steps, then Polly herself opened the front door. Her face was flushed red and she wore a strappy, green sun top, turquoise-blue shorts revealing skinny legs, and flip flops on her feet. Distractedly, she pushed her hair back from her face with both hands. 'Yes?' she said blankly, then recognition dawned in her eyes. 'Oh,' she said. 'The Lost Property Office. What are you doing here?' She peered up and down the road, as if expecting a team of LPO people to be lurking nearby.

'I'm Natalia O'Shea. We talked on Baker Street station. Do you remember?'

'Oh, yes, I remember that. You gave me my necklace. It was very kind of you. You didn't get into trouble did you? I wondered if I should've given you some money, a fee. Is that what you've come for?' She talked fast, nervously. Her fingernails, Natalia noticed when she pushed back her hair, were worse-bitten than before, the skin red and raised around the bases of the nails.

'No, nothing like that,' Natalia reassured

her. 'I just wanted to talk to you about the evening you lost your necklace. Can you remember anything at all about that night out?'

Polly shook her head. 'All I remember was standing in *The Glass and Bottle* pub between Camden and Mornington Crescent, drinking and talking, the rest is blank. I must have drunk more than usual.'

'Can I come in and talk about it?'

'Oh, do we have to? The flat's a bit of a mess. I haven't had time to tidy.' Polly glanced back inside.

'There's something about that night you need to know.'

'Oh. Oh, OK.' Something flickered in Polly's green eyes. Natalia's words had struck a chord. She stood back. 'You'd better come in then.'

Polly's hallway had the original Victorian tiles on the floor, some broken and uneven. The walls were painted a dull cream.

'We really ought to get the landlord to do something about it,' she said apologetically.

As she entered the long room that ran from front to back, the dividing wall having long ago been turned into an arch, she could see why Polly hadn't wanted to invite her inside. The walls and skirting were painted white, the floor wood laminate, but it was hard to see them as every surface, and most of the floor, was covered, partly with magazines and papers, but mainly with swatches of material, lace, ribbons and buttons.

'I'm a costume designer,' Polly said, rushing Natalia past the laden dining table, into the tiny kitchen to the left, then through the open back door. 'Freelance. I work from home, as you can see. Let's go in the garden. How's about a drink?'

'A cup of tea would be lovely,' Natalia said, seeing the bottle and wine glass on the circular, green, iron garden table, the book on the ground beside Polly's chair.

While Polly busied herself in the kitchen Natalia looked around the small garden. Like the indoors, it was not a tidy garden, but she could see that this was where Polly poured her love and expressed herself. The grass in the centre was rough and long, but on either side borders overflowed with flowering plants and the little concrete patio was ringed with pots of herbs, geraniums and marigolds, all coming into flower, their bright colours imparting their cheerful energy to the tiny space.

'Here you are.' Polly plonked a mug on the table and then plonked herself on the other chair, poured herself some more wine and picked up the glass. 'Cheers,' she said, and drank, but there was a wariness in her eyes.

'How long have you lived here?' Natalia asked.

'Five years. My gran used to live in one of those mansion blocks nearer the shops. She claimed one of her admirers had bought it for her, but when she died I found it was rented. Maybe he paid her rent for her for a while. She's the reason I moved to this part of London. This place is rented, too. I don't see myself ever being able to buy a place.'

'You've no other family?'

'Just my dad in Australia. A few cousins and ancient aunts and uncles scattered in the country.'

Natalia thought of her mother and father, of her brothers and sisters, and wider extended family. How they'd seen her through her darkest days when her son had been kidnapped, and helped Dermot when he'd come to lodge with them. Polly might have good friends, or be a loner by nature, but had her attacker been able to sense a vulnerability there, no one to check up on her, no one to back her up?

'Polly,' she said gently. 'I'm going to ask you something. Please don't take it the wrong way. I only want to establish what is happening, to try and prevent other woman from suffering your experience. The night you lost the necklace. Do you think you might have been sexually assaulted? Because that has happened to at least one other woman in the same area who, like you, can remember nothing of the event itself. And, I believe, more women have suffered this, too.'

'Oh, God!' Polly stared at her aghast, then rubbed her hand across her freckled face, making her fair skin even redder. 'I ... I've put it out of my mind. Didn't want to believe it. Too awful to think it might've happened.' She took a shuddering breath, closed her eyes, then opened them again. 'But I have these dreams, nightmares, and then... Yes, I think I was. But how could I tell anyone? It was bad enough to get so drunk I lost my necklace, but to be in such a state that I picked up some bloke, let him have his jollies, and then get back here somehow, god knows how, and not remember a thing. That's embarrassing. Walking disaster area, me.'

'Polly, try not to be so hard on yourself.' Natalia leaned forward. 'I remember you had healing scratches and grazes on your arms. Did you have any other injuries?'

Polly groaned. 'I did. My back was sore and scraped – what a picture *that* paints – but who knows? I could've been falling over drunk. I could've been all over this bloke, asked him to go with me. How do I know? But I can't pretend any more. I know something happened. There were tell-tale stains and I was physically very sore.' She shuddered again. 'It's funny. I think I've put it out of my mind, and then I find myself thinking about it. Obsessing. Did it really happen? Did anyone see? Where did it happen? I feel dirty. Like I'm kind of soiled.'

'Polly, you've had a horrible experience. Have you been to a doctor? If you don't want to go to your surgery, there are special clinics that are very discreet. I hate to say this, but you must be checked.'

Polly gave a sob and covered her face, hunching forward. When she spoke, her voice was muffled, strangled, as if forced through an aching throat. 'That's what I didn't want to face up to. Supposing it was unprotected ... I've got some ... awful disease. Am I such a bad person ... to be punished this way?'

'Polly ... Polly, look at me,' Natalia said fiercely, and when Polly raised her tear-blotched face to her she said, 'You are not a bad person and it is not your fault. It's *his* responsibility, the man who did this to you. The other woman I mentioned. She was assaulted, she went to the police, and when her blood was analysed, traces of Rohypnol were discovered. She'd been drugged, then sexually assaulted.'

She'd received Jason's call that day, saying that the lab tests had confirmed the presence of the drug in the woman's blood.

'Ohmigod, do you think that's what happened to me, and that's why I can't remember anything?' A range of pained emotions crossed Polly's face.

'I do. It's very powerful and the effect lasts for hours, especially if you've had a lot of alcohol.'

Shamefaced, Polly looked at the wine she was drinking. 'Thing is, there have been one or two times when I've blacked out before, can't remember much the next day. I suppose I get carried along with the crowd. It's what everyone does of a Saturday or Friday night. Although I did think this was different, how could I be sure? If I went to the police, they might ask around and people would say, yeah, I've seen Polly really blotto on occasions.'

'You must stop beating yourself up. It's

this man. He has undermined your self-confidence, your belief in yourself. You are questioning your whole life now, and you must stop. We must focus on this one night, this one incident.'

Polly gave a watery smile. 'Thanks. I suppose I needed a good talking to. Oh, there I go again, don't I.' She paused. 'But you're so right about the confidence thing. I ... I haven't been out since that night, not to clubs or pubs or anywhere. I went to a friend's house for supper, got a taxi back. I feel like I can't trust myself ... or anyone else.'

Natalia swallowed the last of her tea. 'I know it's a lot to ask, but could you tell me everything you can remember about that night. Even the smallest details could help. Better still, could you show me?'

18

From outside *The Glass and Bottle* looked like your typical Victorian London pub, with dark, red-and-green ceramic tiles lining part of the outside walls. Hanging baskets spilled bright trails of busy lizzies, petunias and fuchsias above punter's heads outside. Situated on the corner off a small cul de sac and the main Camden High Street drag, people stood outside, or sat on the pavement and in the narrow cobbled cul de sac itself.

Touching Polly's arm, Natalia looked at her concerned. 'Are you OK? We don't have to go in there, if you don't want.'

'No, we must. I need to know what happened that night, and this is the last place I remember. In a way, it's a relief to talk about it, when it's just in your head it all seems so much bigger and more terrifying.'

'So you were here Friday two weeks ago?' Natalia gently nudged.

Polly took a deep breath, as if about to swim underwater, and sat up straighter. 'Yeah. As I said, I was out with my girl friend, Sal. There're a few different places we like to go to, especially one in Camden Lock, but it was closed for a private function, so we started walking along Camden Road towards Mornington Crescent. We loved being able to walk along without coats. It was still light, so it couldn't have been more than nine, half nine. We saw *The Glass and Bottle*.'

Looking up at the pub, Polly's flow of words suddenly dried up.

Pushing open the door, Natalia held it open for Polly. 'Ready?'

Polly nodded, squeezing Natalia's arm in gratitude, 'Thank you. I never would have had the guts to confront this alone. If there's a chance one of the bartenders might recognise me, then I've got to try, right?'

Her face screwed up in determination, Polly pushed through into the bar. Inside, the pub was half empty and it was a completely different story to its old-fashioned facade. Carpets had been stripped away and replaced with the ubiquitous light-blond, laminate wood flooring. Chrome-legged bar stools with bright-red, retro vinyl seats lined the bar, which was coated with wood veneer. There were traditional beer pumps drawing every type of beer from real ale to imported lagers. The wall behind was mirrored up to the ceiling and glass shelving was laden with every kind of spirit and mixer, lined up ready to make the list of cocktails advertised, including the Pink Fairy that Polly's friend Sal had been drinking the night they'd been there.

Natalia listened as Polly surveyed the room, remembering. 'It was heaving. People were sitting out on the pavement and inside was full. We stood at the bar. I was on vodka,

Sal was drinking Pink Fairies, when her mobile went. It was her sister Sara calling – from the maternity ward! Of course, Sal wanted to go and see her immediately. She wanted me to come, too, but I said no – you go on your own. I thought it would be a bit awkward, the first visit, with me there. I'd see her next time.'

Overhead, big, wooden Raffles-style fans lazily swirled the air-conditioned atmosphere around, more for effect than purpose. They approached the bar. It was two weeks since Polly had been to this pub on a chance visit. She wasn't a regular. Would any of the bartenders serving today have been on duty that night, and if so, would they recognise her? Her hair and colouring were quite distinctive, which might help.

'I decided to stay and finish my drink, chill out, you know. Yes, I remember, the bartender said, here, have another on the house to celebrate. So I did. It was a good atmosphere in there. And then ... then I got chatting to this bloke. He seemed really nice, easy to talk to, and he bought me a drink. And after that, that's when it goes all hazy – a sort of blur. You can't tell if you remember something real, or you're making it up. Like you're seeing a few glimpses of things that make no sense. And when I woke up, I felt terrible. I was lying in the hallway outside my flat, and everything hurt. Thank goodness it was early, so I got inside before my neighbour upstairs saw me.'

'What can you remember about the man who bought you the drink?'

Polly frowned, concentrating. 'He said his name was Fred. I made some joke about that, I said it's an old-fashioned name these days, and he laughed and said he was an old-fashioned kind of guy. He was, well, ordinary-looking in a nice kind of way. Dark hair, medium build. Not the sort of man I go for, but he was very easy to chat to. It can't have been him, surely?' she said almost wistfully. 'He seemed nice, and he seemed to like me. You know what it's like, your drink's on the bar, you turn around, you go to the loo, you don't watch it all the time. Anyone could've drugged it. Even one of the bar staff.'

'Did you tell Fred where you lived? Give him your address? I'm not saying it's him, if you don't think it is, but someone else could've overheard.'

'No way. I know my way around – or I thought I did. You don't give your address or phone number to anyone till you're sure of them. But when I was drugged, who knows what I said.'

'Might your address have been in your handbag?'

'I carry just a purse on a night out, thin strap, over the shoulder, with just a bit of cash and a credit card with not much credit on it, bit of make-up, and my door keys. Why are you asking about my address?'

'I was wondering how you got home and inside your own front door. If everything was a blur and on this drug you probably wouldn't be able to even walk properly. It's another part of the puzzle to sort out.

'Now, it's a bit earlier than when you were here two weeks ago, but the bartenders are probably here all evening. Do you recognise any of them? Are you ready to start asking questions?'

Polly nodded vigorously. 'Absolutely. Do it now, while I'm feeling strong and angry.' She slid off her stool and looked at each of the bartenders in turn. All the young men and women wore white shirts with rolled-back sleeves, and black waistcoats and trousers. 'That one, I'm sure he served me that night. I remember asking where he was from and he said Lithuania.'

The young man in question was tall, with

a prominent forehead and pale-brown hair cut very short. Natalia caught his eye. Fortunately, there was a bit of a lull, and so he came straight over.

'Drinks, ladies?' he asked.

'Two bottles of sparkling mineral water, thanks,' Natalia said, looking towards Polly.

Polly nodded her agreement. The bartender returned, poured the water into glasses and they paid for their drinks.

'May we ask you a question?' Natalia began. 'My friend was in here exactly two weeks ago. You served her. Do you remember her at all? We're trying to find the man she was drinking with.'

'Ah, lonely hearts,' the bartender answered. Natalia thought it easier not to correct his misapprehension for now. 'No, I'm sorry. So many people. If you come many times, yes, but once? No. Not even pretty woman.' He smiled charmingly.

'Can you ask your workmates if they remember Polly at all?' Natalia asked.

'Sure. I'll ask.'

He went away and Polly made a wry grimace. 'I don't get the impression that pretty ladies are what interest him, but even if I was a young man I can see it'd be hard to remember one person out of all the thousands they serve. I wouldn't, if it was me.' She took a drink, slopping some as she put the glass down. Natalia saw her hand was shaking. 'This is probably hopeless, isn't it. May as well go home.'

'Give yourself time,' Natalia reassured her. 'Look around the bar, the room. Picture yourself here two weeks ago. Can you think back to when you and your friend Sal were at the bar? Where were you standing?'

Polly looked up and down the bar, then said, 'We were along there by the cash till.' Natalia slid off her stool and they walked to where Polly indicated. 'I remember the till because one woman was trying to pay by debit card. It was her hen night and she was too drunk to remember her pin number.' She grinned at the recollection. 'The bartender had a ponytail – that's him down there – he said he'd take her name and address and they could sort it out later, but she kept giving him the name of her honeymoon hotel!'

While Polly continued to talk, Natalia tried to catch the attention of the young man whose wavy, brown hair was tied back into a ponytail.

'Then Sal went and I was standing here, listening to the music, leaning back against the bar like this.' She turned her back to the bar. 'And then Fred was beside me. He was buying a drink, but I didn't see who served him.'

'Had you noticed him before?'

Polly shook her head. 'He's not really the sort of bloke you'd notice, in my view. Sort of medium everything. He was wearing a green shirt and black trousers. He was sort of crinkly around the eyes. He didn't try to chat me up, just talked about the music, the crowd, that sort of thing. Oh!' She clutched Natalia's arm. 'I've just remembered, when I finished my drink, I had to go to the loo and he said, "Don't forget to come back. When you do, there'll be another one waiting for you."'

The bartender with the ponytail approached them. 'What can I get you?'

'Nothing, thanks, but do you recognise my friend? She was here two weeks ago. You were serving a woman who kept giving you the name of her honeymoon hotel, when you were trying to get her to pay.'

The man smiled. 'I remember the hen night, but that distracted me. Love to help but–' He shrugged and held his hands wide, then moved on.

Polly sighed. 'I don't seem to make much

of an impression, do I?'

'You made one on me,' Natalia said. 'What about the bartender who gave you the free drink on the house when Sal was still here?'

'That was a woman, blonde. I don't see her here tonight.'

'Let's go to the ladies and see if that jogs any memories.'

Together, they crossed the floor and went through a large, heavy fire door into a narrow corridor painted cream with a floor of small, red tiles. In the dim light Natalia could just make out a fire-exit door at the far end, with the gents first and then the ladies. They pushed their way into the one marked 'Ladies'.

It was a surprisingly large room, tiled largely in black marble and containing a row of four cubicles. In one corner, beside the washbasins, stood a jug of flowers, purple irises and white gypsophila. The surfaces around the basins were spotlessly clean.

'I remember thinking when I came in, cor, these are better than your usual pub loos,' Polly remarked.

'Thank you.' A small woman dressed in blue overalls, over a T-shirt and purple crimplene trousers, emerged from the furthest cubicle, carrying a mop and bucket. Her scraggle of hair had turned a ferociously unnatural orange colour and she wore long, dangling earrings. 'I do me best. There's not enough folk take pride in their work like what I do.'

'I remember you!' Polly said. 'I remember your earrings.'

'Ta.' The woman peered at Polly. 'You look familiar an' all. When was this?'

'Friday evening two weeks ago. I came in here, thought this is nice, then that's when I must've blacked out.' Polly paused. 'Was I sick? I felt all queasy, like being on a fairground ride. I don't recall going in to one of the loos but ... oh no, I do remember looking up at the lavatory bowl. I must've been on the floor.'

'That's right.' The small woman gave the throaty laugh of a lifelong smoker. 'I'd just done me second clean of the night – 'bout ten it was – done the loo rolls and was wiping off the basins when you stumbled in, went in the loo, sat down on the seat with the door open, only the lid was down.' She cackled. 'Swore something terrible, you did, got up, banged the door to. I thought, she's had a skinful already. Of course, that's what made me do it.'

'Do what?' Natalia asked.

'Leave me fags behind. I did the gents, then come back in to fetch them. There was a queue of girls by then and one said to me 'ere, can't you get that door open, she's been in there an age. I bent down and saw you was slumped half on the floor.'

Polly groaned and hid her face in her hands.

'Don't worry,' Natalia said. 'It was the drug. It was not your fault.'

'Drugs, was it? Wouldn't surprise me. The things I see in here.'

Natalia didn't bother to correct her, respecting Polly's privacy. 'What happened next?'

'Bloke comes to the door. The girls are all laughing and complaining. Seen my girlfriend? 'e says. I said is that her in there? He looked and said, yes. Lucky her dress was down and her knickers up.' She cackled again. 'I found you hadn't locked the door, so it was easy to get you out. You was moaning and your eyes were rolling up in your head. I says you can take her out the side door to get some fresh air quick. Thanks, 'e said.'

'That could have been Fred.'

Polly looked up. 'Yes, I think I remember that bit. Dustbins, some ... some boxes?

Crates? I couldn't stand up properly, my legs were all wobbly, and I went down on my knees. That gave me a close-up of the gutter. There was a broken drain.'

Thanking the attendant, Natalia turned to Polly, 'We can go outside and take a look.'

Outside the ladies, they pushed at the fire-exit door, which yielded easily and they stepped outside. They were at the top end of the cul de sac. On their right were high, black-painted wooden gates with lethal metal spikes along the top to deter thieves. Opposite them was a windowless, yellow-brick wall. To the left and right, on both the narrow pavement and on the road, stood black rubbish bags, empty beer crates, big metal canisters, and folded cardboard. Above, the sky was darkening, with a few black shapes of clouds looming.

'Look there,' Natalia said. 'There is your broken drain.'

The heavy-duty metal grille set into the gutter, flush to the kerb, was indeed missing a corner. Polly looked at it and shivered. 'Makes me feel sick all over again, looking at it. So I'm standing here with Fred support-ing me. It has to be him, doesn't it?' she said to Natalia.

'Looks like it. Who else would know you

were in the ladies and come looking for you?'

'Unless someone else spiked my drink, and they followed us and when I parted company with Fred they ... no, that's too far-fetched.'

'From here, with this man supporting you, you would have had to go back past the entrance, there's no other way out. I'm sure if he'd taken you back inside, someone would've remembered... What's that?'

She was looking towards the pub entrance. She saw a man stepping out backwards, feeling his foot over the brass lip of the door lintel to the pavement outside. As he moved out more fully, she saw he was supporting a woman. He had one arm round her waist, she had one arm round his neck and was lolling against him.

As he half-dragged, half-carried the woman out of view towards Camden High Street, Polly and Natalia looked at each other in horror. Could they be witnessing Polly's attacker dragging away his next victim?

Fighting their way through a knot of revellers staggering out of the pub heading for the nearest curry house, by the time they turned the corner, the man and woman had disappeared.

'Which way did they go?' Polly asked,

puffing slightly. Although clouds were gathering in the sky and a blustery wind had started up, swirling about old chip wrappers, empty polystyrene burger boxes and discarded plastic bottles, the night air was humid and heavy.

Suddenly the crowd cleared, and there he was, heading in the direction of Mornington Crescent station.

The two women set off in pursuit. Medium was how Polly had described Fred. This man was medium build. About five foot ten or eleven, Natalia guessed from this distance. She had seen his hair in the light from the pub, and it was a mid brown, and seemed neatly cut. As they hurried along, despite having heavy limbs from the humidity, Natalia screwed up her eyes to see more in the lights from passing cars and from streetlamps, which had just come on. The man was wearing some sort of jacket and dark trousers or jeans. Again, nothing that stood out in any particular way.

'Do you think it's Fred?' she asked, panting now.

'Hard to tell ... could be. But I need to see his face.'

Natalia was sure Polly must be feeling her own concern for the woman at his side. He seemed to be jerking her along. Her legs made spasmodic movements, as if trying to walk, her feet occasionally touching the ground. He tightened his grip around her waist, his other hand holding on to the arm around his neck. He had her in a semi-fireman's lift. Long, dark hair flowed around her shoulders and over onto his. Her head would fall and then suddenly snap back up again. She was thin, and that enabled him to move at speed.

'We're gaining on him,' Polly said.

'We must catch him before he gets through the barriers, if he's going into the station.'

They broke into a faster trot as they saw him stop at the pedestrian lights that led across the road to the triangular traffic island in the middle of the road, where the High Street divided to flow either side of the tube station. On the left was the black exterior of Koko, the popular nightclub, on the right a residential street began. The station stood at the end of its row of buildings like the prow of a ship.

'Fred' dragged his companion across, dodging between a car and a taxi. Stepping out into the street, Natalia had to haul Polly back as a large, articulated lorry turned the corner.

As soon as it was gone, both women launched themselves across the road, earning a short blast of the horn from a car driver. As 'Fred' went inside the wide entrance of the station, Natalia sprinted ahead of Polly. He must not get through the barriers.

Turning into the station, the big metal security gate that was pulled across when the tube was closed, was folded back concertina fashion. The hall itself was lined with cream tiles inset with maroon.

Quickly, Natalia took in her surroundings. There was a small ticket window with a brass tray beneath for the exchange of tickets and money, surrounded by dark-brown wood. In front of it, a 'wet floor' sign. Opposite it a small, gold plaque commemorated the Northern Line Centenary of the opening of the Charing Cross, Euston and Hampstead Railway in 1907.

And there was the man, the girl at his side leaning awkwardly against him as he fumbled in his pocket for his Oyster card. He pressed it to the electronic pad and as the gates opened began to push her through.

'No!' Natalia cried. 'Stop!' and she grabbed hold of the woman's arm, pulling her back.

'What the fuck?' The man turned on her.

19

'You've buggered up my card, you silly cow.'

The woman, knees buckling under her, came to, blinking heavily kohled eyes at Natalia. 'Wos goin' on? Who the bleedin' hell is this silly mare. Girlfriend of yours?' she laughed.

Behind her, Natalia could hear the thunder of Polly's heels on the hard floor as she raced to catch up.

'Shut it, Mel babe, will ya? What's your game then?' he glared aggressively at Natalia.

'No good going after his wallet – he ain't got one. Ha Ha!' Mel wobbled and the man grabbed her. Already Natalia knew they had the wrong man. These two people obviously knew each other very well.

'Were you in *The Glass and Bottle* two weeks ago today?'

'So what if he was?' Mel started before the man could speak. 'Free country, ain't it? Who are you? You ain't cops, I can tell that much.'

'Why do you want to know?' he asked.

217

Polly was shaking her head and pulling at Natalia's arm. But if he had been there, maybe he saw something. It was worth asking.

'Do you recognise this woman?' she asked. 'She was assaulted that night and we're looking for witnesses–'

'You leave my husband alone, d'you hear?' Mel raised her handbag to hit Natalia. Fortunately, she was too squiffy to strike properly and started staggering backwards. 'You leave my Dave alone,' she shrieked, flailing her bag. 'He wouldn't hurt anyone.'

'I'm sorry,' Natalia held up her hands. 'I wasn't accusing him of anything.'

'Everything all right?' A young woman in her twenties, wearing the pale-blue London Transport jacket with yellow reflective stripe, had emerged from a brown wooden door. Natalia was aware that she had been observing them through the plate glass window of her office there.

'I'm just trying to get my wife home, now this silly mare has ruined me Oyster,' Dave, the man who was not Fred, explained about touching in but not touching out. The official led him over to the luggage gate.

'You can go through this way, sir,' she said, while Natalia and Polly retired to one side of the entrance hall.

'Are you all right?' Polly asked anxiously, as Dave and Mel got through the barriers and turned left for the lifts to the platforms. 'I'm so sorry. It's all my fault.'

'You must stop blaming yourself,' Natalia commanded. 'I chose to go up to them. He was the wrong man, but we had to try.'

Mel and Dave dealt with, the female official turned back to them.

'Can I help you? My name's Claire. I'm the station assistant here.'

'I was here a fortnight ago, about the same time, maybe later? I was probably drunk. There was a man?' Polly said.

Claire shook her head, 'Love, I must see hundreds like that in an hour.'

Natalia suddenly remembered something Najjah had said. 'There's another entrance, isn't there? The way the cleaners come in?'

'That's outside and around the other side. A black door. They usually work from about eleven at night till five in the morning.'

'Thanks,' Natalia said. 'Come on, Polly, let's take a look.'

They walked outside onto the Hampstead Road and then around the corner. In Eversholt Street they saw the back of the station was brick and stone with a black wooden inset. In that inset there was a door, with a lock. This must be the entrance the cleaners used.

'What about here?' Natalia asked.

Polly sighed despondently. 'I am getting some flashbacks – like being inside the station, the tiling, the hard concrete floor, the stairs.'

'If only we knew the timing. If you were taken in the front after the station closed, the metal security gate would be locked, and there are houses all around. Someone would notice it being opened, surely. But here there's only that big block opposite, the Crowndale Centre, which looks as if it's not in use. Fred could have used this back door to get you down to platform level, or back up again. But then the cleaners would be in here and they would have heard you, surely.'

'But why? Why not have his way with me in the bushes somewhere?' Polly flapped her arms helplessly. 'Why go through all this effort, dragging a half senseless woman along the street and into the Underground?'

'If I'm right, and I'm more sure than ever now, this man, probably Fred, is doing the same action over and over again. It's an obsession and he will have his rituals. They will all mean something to him, this station

220

must have some significance to him.'

Heading back inside the station, Natalia made to head towards the barriers, Polly a step ahead of her, when Polly came to an abrupt halt.

'What is it?' Natalia asked, drawing alongside, but Polly was already veering left towards the luggage barrier.

'I remember this. I remember going through here. I never use this station but I remember this.' Natalia watched as the colour drained from Polly's face. Polly clutched Natalia's arm. 'Parts of it are coming back to me. Like the broken drain, and this. I remember his hand sweeping a card over here.' Polly's fingers brushed over the magnetic disc on the barrier, before covering her face, hot tears erupting.

20

The last place Natalia wanted to be today was on an LPO outing. Only here she was, along with half the LPO team, being driven down High Holborn in a minibus. Imposing buildings lined either side of the clogged thoroughfare, their upper storeys just visible above the tops of big, leafy trees. The windscreen wipers on the minibus kept up a rhythmic clacking, and the driver had the air vents on full blast, making conversation impossible. For, at last, the hot, blustery wind and the dark, ominous clouds had given way to a downpour of rain that had started in the night and didn't look like letting up any time in the near future. Huge raindrops bounced off the street and steam rose from the bonnet of the minibus as the heat of the engine evaporated the cool rain.

It was the day Donna had volunteered them to take part in a simulated Underground rescue operation and the Lost Property Office was going to be manned for the day by Ranjit's team. They were to be bussed somewhere in central London for some special training underground.

'I bet she's hoping Area Commander Jonathan Crane will be practising his lifesaving skills on her,' Mark leaned in and murmured into Natalia's ear. 'Bit of mouth to mouth, that's what she's after.'

One side of the bus had a row of single seats, and Avon, Stefan, and Cliff sat on those, still not talking to each other since the hooter incident. Cliff stared morosely out of the bus window chewing nicotine-substitute gum, while Stefan listened to his i-pod and Avon loudly rustled the pages of her Metro newspaper. Natalia and Mark were seated side by side, a few seats behind Donna and Rose.

Natalia took the chance of turning round and saying to Mark, 'She'll be expecting to get a gold star for volunteering us, I'm sure. Do you know where we are going?'

'Search me. Still, a day away from our desks. Can't be bad.'

The minibus pulled up at the bottom of High Holborn, just around the corner into the left arch of the Aldwych.

'Follow me,' Donna announced.

'Is Donna tour guide now?' Stefan asked, hanging back as they clambered down from the bus, to join Mark and Natalia. The women put up umbrellas, the men turned up their coat collars, and they squelched their way across the bottom of High Holborn, following the curve of the Aldwych. Ahead, lay the impressive entrance of the Waldorf Hotel, and across the way a large, old church that also fronted the Strand before it turned into Fleet Street.

Just past the Waldorf, Donna came to a stop outside a boarded-up area, with a door in it, saying, 'This is one of the old entrances to the Aldwych station. It was once part of the Piccadilly Line, but it's not in public use any more. That means the Met can use it for training purposes. Down we go.'

A policeman, manning the door, checked their IDs, one by one, and let them in.

Once inside, they descended a few steps. Donna indicated to Cliff to open the metal gates of a big, square service lift. Then they all obediently crammed in. Cliff slammed the doors shut, put the safety catch in place, and pressed the button to start the lift.

'I'm feeling all caged in,' Mark said, as it sank slowly deeper and deeper underground.

'Now I know what a battery hen feels like,' someone behind them remarked.

'My feet are soaking,' Natalia heard Avon complain. 'My toes are sore.'

'Will there be food and drink down there?' Cliff asked.

'What about smoking?' Stefan wanted to know.

'Yes, there will be full catering and no, no smoking, Stefan and Cliff. And Avon, I'm sure there'll be towels to dry off with. Just wait and see.'

Natalia was relieved when the ancient service lift settled at the base of its shaft with a dull thump. Cliff helped Donna pull back the doors and they moved along a short corridor, and then emerged onto what looked like a normal Underground platform. Except that it was full of emergency services' staff, a parade of navy blue and pale blue, black, green, white, and the ubiquitous yellow-and-white safety tabards. There were firemen and women, paramedics, doctors and nurses. There were uniformed policemen and women, as well as British Transport Police and Transport for London staff.

There were also two movie cameras mounted on gantries overhead, each with an operator sitting on a small seat, looking down their lenses and adjusting them.

'This way,' Donna said. 'We'll report in, you can get some coffee, and then it's a case of waiting to be called and told where to lie, sit or stand.'

They trooped after her, still dripping from the rain outside and Avon still complaining about her wet feet. They went through an archway and then into a larger pedestrian hallway, where moving escalators and a central stone staircase led up above. The stairs were set in dark-brown wood, and the familiar red circle and blue cross bar of the

London Underground was mounted at the bottom. Here, chairs were provided and in one corner Natalia saw two make-up women hard at work. They were painting realistic wounds and burns onto the faces and arms of two volunteers.

There was a trolley bearing an urn of tea and one of coffee, with a box of biscuits to one side. Natalia stood in the queue for refreshments, then found herself a chair.

'If this is going to be like making a movie,' Rose said at her side. 'I wish I'd brought a book with me!'

Soon they were joined by Jason and Jack Riley, too.

'This afternoon,' Jack explained, 'we'll have the train moving along the tunnel with the pretend fire raging on board, and then coming into the platform. It's more difficult to deal with.'

'You've done this before?' Natalia asked.

'Not exactly the same, but dealing with crises is part of the training. Can I fetch anyone another drink? Donna, how about you?'

'Thanks, I'll have some coffee.' She was definitely unbending towards him, Natalia thought. 'You know, it must be very difficult tracking people down in a situation like today. How on earth would you know everyone was accounted for? And checking out their addresses and where they live?'

'Going through the eye-witness accounts,' Jason told her. 'It takes a long time, but you have to piece it all together from that. Crosscheck, check, and crosscheck again. What about tracking down addresses, Jack?'

'Not too different from your methods at the Lost Property Office on the whole. Check every item for clues. There are a few other ways, too. You can extract them from Oyster cards, credit cards – it all takes time, but we get there in the end. Natalia, that chair doesn't look too comfortable. Here, take mine.' Before she could protest, Jack had changed places with her. In the process, he placed himself next to Donna. 'Have I left anything out, Donna?'

'Not that I know of,' she shook her head.

'How you finding this?' he asked Jason.

Jason grinned, 'Me, I'd rather be out on our usual patch. Too much hanging about for my liking.'

'Not everywhere's as busy as our patch, Jason,' Jack told him. 'Didn't anyone tell you? Why d'you think we're always doing stop and search up there? Plenty of top brass live around the Camden Town area –

our very own Mr Crane being one of them.'

I wonder, Natalia thought, only half paying attention to the talk buzzing around her. How did the sex attacker find out where his victims lived and deliver them back there? Polly had said she didn't carry her address written down anywhere. An automatic safety precaution, in case her handbag was stolen. Perhaps he did manage to wake them up enough to extract the information. But, as Jack had said, there were other electronic means of finding out addresses. Further proof that she was correct in her surmise. The sex attacker was someone on the inside.

All the while, Natalia could feel the blood draining from her face, trying to keep her thoughts in some order. Across the table, Mark and Jason's footie debate was growing louder and louder. Polly's attacker not only knew the cameras would be down at Mornington Crescent, he also knew when the cleaners took a break. But now there was so much more than that. Gripping the arm of her chair, Natalia touched Jack's arm to get his attention, only for Donna to scowl across at her.

'Jack, would a guard who operates the luggage barrier be able to swipe someone's card and get an address?'

'Nah. Only a member of the London Transport Police has that kind of authorisation,' Jack answered.

'Hey, Natalia, you looking a little pale. Want a top up?' Jason asked, signalling to her empty cup.

Before Natalia could reply, she saw Jonathan Crane coming through the archway from the platform. Donna immediately sat up straighter, calling out to him to come join them.

'We're ready for you, whenever and whatever it is you want us to do, Jonathan,' she said, indicating her staff of nine.

What a bedraggled group we make, Natalia thought. But Jonathan didn't seem to mind what they looked like. Dressed in his uniform, he was very much the Area Commander today, very much in evidence as the senior man.

'Good. I'm here in an observatory capacity today. You've probably noticed the film cameras. We record everything, and then we can watch it over again in minute detail to analyse where we've gone wrong, or where we've gone right, for future reference.' His eyes roved Natalia's colleagues and then came to rest on her. 'It then becomes a useful training tool. The exercise we are going to do today is a fairly minor one, but no less important because of that.'

Natalia was glad when he took his gaze away from her. It was uncomfortably penetrating.

'The scenario is this: a fire has broken out on board a tube train. In the morning, we are going to simulate how we will deal with the fire, and the immediate aftermath – how the emergency services reach the train, that sort of thing. We'll be using dry ice to create 'smoke', so don't be alarmed. It's not the real thing. Then this afternoon we'll be dealing with evacuation procedures, and the moving of injured people.'

Through the arch, Natalia saw a two-carriage tube train amble into the station and come to a halt. Then they were put to work. Natalia was assigned the role of a platform passenger. She walked across, sat down on a bench, took out her newspaper and began to read. All around her, she could hear instructions and discussions, and feel the movement of people bustling to and fro as gradually the scenario was set up. Stefan, Mark and Cliff had become engrossed in the mechanics of the event, while Avon had become equally engrossed with the techniques of making up simulated injuries and burns.

Idly, Natalia started filling in a crossword. Donna or no Donna, if she had an opportunity to talk to the Area Commander today, she would tell him of her new discoveries. Surely he would be the first to want to investigate if one of the men under his command, or within his area, was carrying out sex attacks and using his privileged position to do so?

Her role was soon over, and she, Donna and others were then able, sitting well out of the way, to follow what was happening on TV monitors. Although, Natalia observed the whole time, Donna kept looking from her mobile to the lift door, like there was somewhere else she needed to be. Emergency equipment was broken out on the platform, and used to open the jammed carriage doors and evacuate those within. As she watched, the first foot patrol from above reached the platform – it was Jason, with Detective Sergeant Jack Riley.

In all, the hectic activity went on for over two hours and then it was time to break for lunch. Most people took advantage of the lunch laid on, rather than climb the stairs and go outside. Passing through into another passenger hall, Natalia saw plenty of choice in sandwiches, fruit and cakes laid out on trestle tables. Again, there were urns of tea and coffee on trolleys.

Seeing Donna leave the canteen area and dash for the lifts, Natalia seized her chance and made straight for the Area Commander, who was sitting alone. She'd been waiting for an opportunity like this all morning.

'Area Commander Crane?'

'Jonathan, please,' he corrected, looking up at her from beneath his long lashes, and ushering her to the seat next to his. 'You did well today, Natalia.'

She flushed. So he remembered who she was. Probably because she'd annoyed him by trying to get him to start an investigation. Well, she was about to annoy him all over again.

'I was watching you on the monitor screens. You handled yourself well,' he continued with ease, and smiled. A rather wolfish smile, she thought.

'I didn't have to do much,' she said. 'Donna and Mark contributed more than me.'

'We all had our contribution to offer to make sure it was a hugely successful simulation exercise. It'll probably make the BBC local news, too. We've put out a press release. You might be in it. You looked good on the screen.'

'Thanks. Mr Crane–'

'Jonathan, please.' He smiled again and she became aware of his powerful thigh pressing against hers.

Natalia glanced around. Rose sat reading a book, and on the other side Mark and Stefan were deep in conversation. Cliff and Avon sat alone at separate tables, while Jason and Jack were chatting merrily with a group of friends from the BTP on the other side of the canteen.

'Do you remember me telling you about the sex attacker?' she said.

'Yes, I haven't forgotten any of our meetings. Mornington Crescent, wasn't it?'

She remembered Jack saying that Crane lived near there, but he didn't mention it. 'I have more information now. I spoke to one of the station staff, and from what she tells me this man must be able to get into restricted areas using a pass card or keys. He has to be someone working with London Transport in some way.'

'I see,' he nodded thoughtfully. 'You've really followed this up, haven't you. Well, if you think there's a case to be investigated, then I'd like to hear more.'

Unfortunately, just then the bell rang for the afternoon exercises. Jonathan covered her hand. 'Perhaps we can find an opportunity to speak about this later. Perhaps over a drink?' He pulled his hand away as Mark and Stefan loped over.

'You ready, Nat?'

21

Ten minutes later, six of the Lost Property Office team – Donna, Avon and Cliff, Natalia, Stefan and Rose – were seated in the same area in the same carriage, designated as train passengers. Today, everyone, like Natalia, was dressed in old jeans, T-shirts and shirts. Outside, the rain had stopped overnight and the day was cooler and brighter, but with showers forecast. However, that was not why they were dressed in their oldest clothes. Jonathan had warned them that they might be required to walk along the tunnel.

Bang! It was like a crack, followed by a brief rumble, and then the station immediately began to fill with smoke. Even though she knew that a device had not detonated, that a fire had not started, still Natalia found herself jumping to her feet and looking around wildly. Alarms began to wail, as London Transport employees began running through the smoke, shouting commands. She had a confused image of the occupants of the train carriage, face pressed against the window, and then was following commands to 'clear the area, clear the area!'

There was a bright flash, followed by an intense, high-pitched sound, then a second blinding flash followed by three loud, percussive bangs. The Underground carriage screeched to a halt, full brakes applied. If it had been travelling at normal speed, passengers would have been hurled from one end of the carriage to the other. The lights flickered and died, and there were several gasps around them.

'Don't worry, Natalia,' Stefan said at her side. 'It's not real. Are you OK?' he asked Rose, sitting on his other side. Natalia noticed that she had automatically crossed herself when the train halted. She must be Roman Catholic.

The voice of the train driver was heard over the tannoy.

'I need to ask everyone to evacuate the

train. There is a risk of fire. I repeat, evacuate the train immediately. Carriage A, your doors have jammed and you will need to use the emergency procedures to open them. The live rail is not, I repeat not, live so you will be safe.'

'Which carriage are we?' Avon asked, jumping up in agitation, as usual having paid more attention to her own concerns than what was going on around her. 'Are we A? I think I feel claustrophobic. I want to get out.'

Any panic Natalia may have been feeling was quickly diffused by the animated voices of her colleagues in the dark. She smothered an affectionate smile.

'We're carriage B,' Donna told her. 'There's nothing to worry about. Now, when we get out, I want us to stick together. I've got to pretend to fall over and get a nasty gash on my arm, and we'll bind it up. I'll show you what to do.'

'What happens to me?' Avon wanted to know. 'Do I twist my ankle?'

'Nothing happens to you. You have to walk beside the rails towards the station.'

'I can be helping you,' Avon decided, finding a role for herself and in the process forgetting her claustrophobia.

The doors began to open jerkily. Some of the other volunteers clustered at the gap, teetering, before jumping down onto the rails, then the ground. Donna held her team back until everyone else was gone.

'We'll check to make sure everyone is out,' she said. 'Make sure no children are hiding anywhere.'

They made a show of looking through the carriage.

'We are the brave ones,' Stefan said. 'With our stiff upper lips.' He flapped his lips at Mark, who responded in kind.

'Come on,' Donna sighed. 'The fare-dodging, non-English speaker must be in the other carriage. Time to go.'

Cliff went first, then the other men. Natalia, with her long legs, felt confident jumping down, but Crane held out his arms to catch her anyway. Behind her, she could hear Stefan call out to Rose, too, who followed her. Avon was next.

'Are you sure there's no electricity down there?' she asked.

'Look,' Mark said. 'I'm standing on the live – aargh!' He pretended he was being electrocuted.

'How childish,' Avon said, and climbed down awkwardly. Donna followed, simulating a nasty fall. In the dark, Cliff and Avon used their clothing to bind her arm.

'Which way now? I've lost track,' Avon said.

'It's this way,' Cliff told her, pointing down the tunnel. 'Everyone else has gone that way.'

'OK, Cliff, you take one side and I'll take the other. It's OK, Donna, we've got you.'

She was back to her bossy self. What's more, Natalia thought, she wasn't trying to keep her distance from Cliff. Could his no-smoking policy be doing the trick?

She found herself falling in just behind Rose. Stefan, ahead of them, tested the way, as the two women walked beside the rails. In the semi-darkness, that close, she couldn't be certain, but she thought she saw Stefan holding Rose's hands.

Ah, little brother, she thought, Ah.

'Here come the emergency services,' Stefan told them.

Up ahead, where they could before make out the faint glimmer of the station, were both helmet-mounted and hand-held flash-lights, and shouting voices, moving steadily towards them. They were checking each person they met, giving instructions, passing them on down the line.

Before Natalia could reply, she heard someone behind her say, 'Excuse us, can we get past? We've got an unconscious man here.'

The two women flattened themselves against the curved wall of the tunnel. Natalia could feel the rough brickwork digging through her shirt. How old would those bricks be, she wondered. How old was the dust clinging to them?

Two men had made a makeshift stretcher with some coats. Between them, they were carrying Mark, whose eyes were closed, his hands crossed on his chest. Just as he passed the girls he opened his eyes and winked, wiggling his fingers at them. 'Are we nearly there yet?' he asked.

'Shut it, or we'll leave you here,' one of the men replied, laughing.

Separated from Rose, the others up ahead, Natalia stumbled, losing her footing, only for a pair of strong arms to reach out and steady her. Up close, she could smell his aftershave. Jonathan.

His hand was on her bare arm. He was looking down at her flesh as he ran his fingertips down over her skin towards her hand. Then he looked into her eyes. She could read his sexual interest very clearly.

'Why don't we arrange to get together?' he suggested. 'Just the two of us.'

'Mr Crane – Jonathan – I'm married,' Natalia said. 'I don't think it would be quite right.'

He raised his eyebrows. 'I've met other married women who think differently.'

'Maybe so, but I'm not one of them. There are plenty of single women who would be very glad of your attention,' she said.

'Give me a married woman every time,' he told her. 'No danger of emotional entanglements there – and more of a challenge. You're a challenge. I knew you would be.'

'I'm sorry, I won't change my mind. I love my husband.'

'I've heard that before, too. Doesn't put a stop to having a bit of fun on the side, does it though?'

'It does in my case,' she told him. 'Don't you want to have a proper relationship?'

'Not at the moment. Oh well, if I can't change your mind–'

'Not about that,' Natalia said, shaking her head. 'In fact, I think it's time we joined the others.'

'Of course,' Jonathan said, but she could still hear the smile in his voice, as he guided her back.

Natalia was relieved to be able to climb back up onto the platform, with full lighting overhead. She blinked, accepted the blanket and cup of tea that a medical volunteer handed her, then went to find the rest of the Lost Property Office team, apart from Donna. Was she being given medical treatment as part of the exercise, Natalia wondered? The others were giving their 'statements' about the incident to Jason, while DS Jack Riley looked on, occasionally correcting Jason, advising him on making his notes correctly, and then finally saying, 'OK, Jason, you've got it now. I think we can give it a rest.'

Just then an excited-looking Donna emerged from the lift. What had she been doing up there, and not down there with the rest of them?

'Great news,' she said. 'I had to go up to get mobile reception.'

'What is it?' Avon asked.

'I've got the flat I was after! I was sharing a rented flat before, but my flatmate is getting married, so I thought why not get my own apartment. And now I have! You'll have to join me after this for a drink – let's have a glass of champagne at Smollensky's on me, to celebrate – you too, Jonathan, if you're free,' she added, seeing him walking towards them.

Stepping away from Natalia, he put his arm around Donna's shoulder, which only made her glow all the more. 'Champagne is a perfect idea,' he said mysteriously, and then added, 'We can toast Donna – *and* her promotion to Liaison Officer between TFL, the BTP and the Met – at the same time.'

'Wow!' Donna squealed. 'You kept that quiet. That's fantastic. I mean...'

Pretty soon, everyone was milling around Donna clapping her on the back and shaking hands with her.

After congratulating Donna, Natalia then excused herself. As she climbed the stairs up to the Strand, she could not help feeling the frustration return, wondering how on earth she was ever going to get someone to take her fears seriously, and investigate on behalf of the women who were being attacked?

22

Natalia saw Dermot was still reading his newspaper, breakfast dishes pushed to one side, when she came into the living room. She'd left early to visit Sunil and Araminda next door before they set off for the hospital, and then returned to have her morning shower.

Dermot looked up. 'What's the news?'

'Sunil tells me that the scans have ruled out a brain tumour. And if it was measles, he would have had the rash by now.'

'That's great news, that is.'

'So it's not measles. But so far the results are inconclusive about epilepsy.'

'Ah.' Dermot rubbed his unshaven chin, enjoying his lazy morning after a long, tough week. 'That would be a life sentence for the wee lad.'

Natalia sat at the dining table and propped her chin in her hand. 'Sunil hopes their baby had some kind of viral infection, and that was what caused the convulsions.'

'It's what the consultant, Mr Kitson, said

was most likely. So what's bothering you? I can tell you're worried.'

'It's Araminda. Ever since that day, she's been a changed woman. She's been so withdrawn. This morning, she was sitting there, just staring into space.'

'Poor woman. She'll probably pick up when their baby's back home again.'

'I hope so. I wanted to do something for her. I was thinking of perhaps asking her to go shopping with me. Or I could sit with her a while.'

'Sure. I daresay she'd be grateful for either of those things.' Dermot's tone was carefully neutral.

'I don't want her to be grateful,' Natalia said. Her tone sounded sharper than she'd intended.

'I didn't think you did.' Dermot's dark-blue eyes were very serious. 'If you want to know what I *really* think, even if you won't like it, I really think she's best left alone. She's coping in her own way, and she has her husband with her and family nearby. She needs time to deal with it.'

'You're probably right. I'm worrying unnecessarily.' Natalia stood up and started clearing the breakfast dishes away. While Dermot continued to read his paper, she put away the clean dishes from the dishwasher and part-filled it with used plates and cups. They'd had their Saturday-morning treat of boiled eggs and lots of toast and butter. During the week, they generally had porridge or muesli and fruit.

As she worked, Natalia remembered Araminda standing by the baby's cradle, rocking to and fro and wailing with grief. Now it was as if she no longer believed her baby was coming home again. What could they do to kindle her hope? She sighed, touching briefly the photos of Nuala, Connor and Paul on the notice board. Then she went back into the living room and took a notepad and pen from the pile of papers on the small coffee table in front of the settee.

'Are we seeing Nuala and Connor this weekend?' she asked. 'I'm just making the shopping list.'

'I told you the other day, they're away out with their mother and Nathan this weekend. Going to the coast somewhere. Come and sit down, relax, put your feet up. I'll make us some coffee, and did I tell you how fetching you always look when you come out of the shower?' he said, snuggling closer. 'Your skin's all pink and your hair's still a wee bit damp.'

'Oh?' she said.

'Yes, very fetching. Don't be worrying about Araminda. Her baby will be fine, babies are very strong. Sure, they're fine wee things!'

Natalia stiffened. Surely Dermot wasn't going to try and persuade her to have their baby, even make a start on it now, at half-past nine on a Saturday morning. She began to feel a wave of panic rising in her. She couldn't deal with it at the moment. Her emotions were still too torn. She didn't know what exactly she felt. But how could she hurt him again?

'And very hard work,' she said, leaning forward away from his embrace and picking up her coffee. 'Never a moment's sleep.'

Rebuffed, Dermot, too, picked up his coffee. 'I wasn't talking about us,' he said.

'Oh.' She dared to look at him. 'I'm sorry.'

'Haven't I done enough, giving you space, not bringing the subject up again? Can't I look at you without you thinking I'm thinking babies?'

'I didn't mean it that way. Oh, what *do* I mean? It's ... you do understand, don't you, Dermot ... it's not about you, or us ... it's Paul. I would feel so ... so guilty...'

'But don't you see that's where you're

wrong! Why would having a baby show you cared less for Paul? Of course it wouldn't.'

'It feels ... it feels as if I'd be giving up on him. As if I didn't believe I'd ever see him again.' As she said it, she realised that that's what had disturbed her about Araminda. She could so easily go that route herself, and give up.

'That's ridiculous, Natalia. It's just the way you're looking at things, and it's the wrong way.'

It was as if the unspoken conversation they'd been having between them for so long, hidden beneath their politeness and caring for each other, had suddenly erupted into the light. And now it was started, it couldn't be stopped, however painful it proved to be.

'Why am I wrong? Am I wrong to still love my son even though ... even though I haven't seen him for six years?'

'You're putting words into my mouth. When have I ever said, stop loving Paul, stop looking for Paul?'

'No, you haven't *said* that, but I think sometimes you're thinking it. Why is she spending all this time on the Internet, it's hopeless.'

'It's your own mind saying that, not me.'

Dermot stood up and began pacing about, running his hands through his hair, making the curls stand out from his head. 'But I think it's something deeper than that. I think it is about us.'

Natalia suddenly felt fear clutch at her heart. What was he saying? Her head began to swim. 'I don't believe you. It's not about us at all.'

'Oh, yes it is. You're not able to go the extra step, make that final commitment. You can't be sure that this is it, this is the one.'

'Dermot!' Natalia jumped up, too. 'I made my wedding vows. I made my commitment to you.'

'Ah, but those are just words. It's what's in here.' He struck his chest above his heart with his fist. 'What do you truly feel in here? To me, it feels like you're holding back. You don't want to give one hundred per cent.'

'Not true!' Natalia hotly denied. 'Haven't I left all my friends and family to live here with you? Make a new life in England?'

'And you're regrettin' it now, aren't you? And blaming me into the bargain. Well, I didn't force you to come.' Dermot shouted the last words. They were both moving about agitatedly. Picking things up and putting them down, straightening and smoothing objects without being aware of what they were doing. Anything to release the tension.

'I chose to come and I *don't* regret it. What are you accusing me of?'

'I've seen you sighing and looking miserable lately, jumping at the least thing – you can't deny it.'

'But that's–' Natalia halted. Somewhere in her mind was a small place that was watching both of them, analysing, assessing. Was Dermot turning into Jem? Was getting angry and shouting and blaming her his attempt to manipulate and bully her into doing what he wanted? Was she fatally attracted to controlling men? Coldness clutched at her heart again. Just who was this man she'd been sharing her life with?

'See, you've got no answer to that. You didn't even want to go away on holiday alone with me. You wanted the kids to come along. What's going on with you, Natalia? You don't talk to me any more, you're shutting me out.'

'I tell you everything that's going on in my life,' she protested. 'Don't tell me I'm keeping secrets from you. Anyway, where's the mystery if I tell you every little thing?'

'You're the mystery. Yes, you tell me all about your work, the goings-on in the office

249

– and chasing after this mythical sex attacker. What's going on there, Natalia?'

'You know what's going on.' Hurting badly, she banged her fist on the dining-room table, making the empty vase on it jump. 'I know that someone is stalking and attacking women. A husband should support his wife!'

'Expectations, you have high expectations, and I'm not meeting them, is that what this is all about? You know what I think?'

No, the voice inside Natalia's head said, I don't want to know, I don't want to hear it, I refuse, see I'm putting my hands over my ears–

'It's avoidance. If you chase after other people's ghosts, you don't have to look at your own life. You're getting hooked on other people's dramas so you don't have to live here, in the present, with me.'

'Rubbish! It's nothing to do with avoiding you. Don't you know what it's like, knowing Jem is in this country, listening out for his voice, thinking I see him around every corner?' She blurted the words out, the thing she hadn't wanted to tell Dermot. In the heat of the moment, all her defences were down, she wasn't in control any more. She had to make him understand.

'That's just what I'm sayin', isn't it! You're hooked on the past, clinging on to it, not moving on with your life. You're still there, with him–'

'No! You can't think I still–'

The insistent ringing of the telephone interrupted the argument.

'Don't answer it,' Dermot said. 'It's probably the neighbours downstairs telling us to shut up. We've got to talk this out.'

'Shout it out, more like! Why are you shouting?'

'This isn't shouting. You want to hear shouting?' He picked up a book and threw it down on the floor.

The phone was still ringing.

Anguished, Natalia turned to the stranger that Dermot had become. 'We have to answer it,' she said.

'Yeah, yeah, I know. Someone might want your help. Anyone else but me. Go on then, do what you must.' Dermot collapsed onto the sofa and buried his head in his hands.

'Natalia, Natalia? Thank God you're there!' It was Rasheda, but her voice was wild, hysterical. 'Oh, God, I don't know what to do.'

'What's the matter? What's going on?'

'It's Ray he … he's outside, right now, can

251

you hear him?'

Natalia thought she could hear faint sounds of yelling.

'I wouldn't let him in. I didn't want him messing up our lives again!' She was sobbing. 'I don't want to go through all that again. I can't!'

'What can you do? Is Jason there?'

Dermot had raised his head and was listening. 'Rasheda?' he mouthed and Natalia nodded.

'No, only Daniel and he ... he's sitting on the stairs crying his eyes out... Oh no! Did you hear that? Ray drop-kicked the front door.'

'If he's trying to break in, you've got to call Jason.'

'No! No! That's just it, I don't want him in my life, in my house, but if the police get involved they'll put him away again. I can't do that to him. And I can't put Jason in such a difficult... Oh shit, he's screaming at my neighbour now. She just put her head out of the window. But I mustn't give in!'

Natalia put her hand over the telephone mouthpiece. 'It's Ray, he's trying to break in. Rasheda wants him gone, but no police,' she told Dermot. 'Rasheda, can you talk to him? Just tell him what you told me. I still think you should call Jason.'

'No way. I no want father and son fighting in the street. Right now they've got a chance, after that, no way. Natalia, I hate to ask but ... is Dermot there? Will he come over and reason with him, man to man?'

23

'Who the hell are you, man? Comin' here, tellin' me what to do?'

Ray was up in Dermot's face the moment they arrived. A wiry man, light on his feet, Ray looked like he'd done a few rounds in a boxing ring in his youth, and still knew a thing or two, as the two men circled around each other.

'I'm not here to tell you what to do. We've got women to do that for us. I just want to talk to you, man to man.'

Huh, Natalia thought, even though she knew Dermot was just trying to lighten up the situation. She stood well back, beside a small rowan tree that was growing in the pavement. Looking up, she could see Rasheda at the window of her first-floor flat.

She'd pushed the sash window up when Dermot arrived so that she could hear what was being said. She looked haggard, her braids awry and not held in place by her usual headband. She was still wearing a silk dressing gown. Raymond must've arrived before she'd even had time to dress.

'Rasheda's my wife's good friend. But I don't want to talk to you about that.'

'No? Well why don't you just piss off and poke your nose in somewhere else. You're not wanted here.' Raymond reached out and gave Dermot a shove in the chest.

Natalia clenched her hands together. Dermot swayed to take the shove, but stood his ground and did not retaliate.

'Look up there,' Dermot said, gesturing to Rasheda and looking up at her for an instant. 'What do you see?'

'What do I see? You kidding me, man? I see a lying, cheating, miserable cow, who won't let her man in the house.'

'Who else do you see?' Dermot's tone was even.

Raymond looked again and his voice softened for a moment. 'Daniel. My gorgeous son, Daniel. Look at him!' His voice hardened. 'The miserable cow won't let me see my son. That's grounds, that is. I'm telling you, that's grounds!'

Natalia leaned forward a little and saw that Daniel was indeed standing beside his mother. His face was solemn, and even from this distance she thought she could see the tracks of tears on his face. Rasheda had her arm around his narrow shoulders. He was so different to Jason, still small for his age, arms and legs all bony. Not too different from his dad, she thought.

'Dad,' he called out now. 'Dad, I didn't know you was coming, I swear.'

'All right, son. That's your mother, that is, lying to you. She's known I was coming out for ages.'

'Listen to me, Raymond,' Dermot was saying. 'Your son Daniel's a sensible boy. Do you really want him to see you like this? I've got a boy, Connor, he's a bit younger, but I wouldn't want him to see me yelling in the street and threatening his mother.'

Raymond pushed his face forward right into Dermot's. 'I ain't threatened his mother. Whoever told you that's lying, I tell you, lying.'

'What you're doing now is threatening enough, don't you think?'

Natalia let out a breath. She'd been afraid Raymond was going to strike Dermot then.

Dermot was right, the street showed plenty of evidence of Raymond's anger. Two dustbins had been knocked or kicked over, their contents strewn across the pavement and into the road. She could see where he'd drop kicked the front door of Rasheda's house, the paint flaking away. When they'd arrived, there had been several groups of neighbours out on the street watching, but all keeping a wary distance. Gradually, they were now walking away in ones and twos, returning to their homes.

Rasheda had lived in this Stoke Newington street for fourteen years, since just before Daniel was born. Some of the other residents had lived here that long, too. No doubt they'd seen Raymond come and go before. Maybe he'd supplied some of them with whatever their current needs were, whether it was a dodgy DVD player, a PlayStation, or maybe some weed.

'I ain't leaving till she lets me in my house,' Raymond stated loudly, looking round to make sure the remaining spectators heard him.

All eyes turned to Rasheda.

'Your house! Your house! Who's been paying the mortgage all these years? It sure ain't you. Who's worked her fingers to the bone to make sure the kids get to school and get fed–'

'Mum, Mum! Don't.' Daniel was pulling at her sleeve. He was right, Natalia thought. Everything Rasheda said was so true, but screaming back at this point could only lead to an escalation of hostility – and it did.

'I've given you money, don't say I haven't, making out I'm the bad guy here. You're trying to keep me from my kids. Or are you saying I'm not their father, eh, eh?'

He was yelling up at Rasheda, surging forward, only held in check by Dermot's hand pressing against his chest. Natalia knew just how strong Dermot was. Working in construction all his life, his muscles were like iron, but he didn't go flaunting it. In fact you wouldn't know, till it came to lifting something, or needing to carry out some job. She'd once seen him pick up a motor-bike that had been blocking the gateway to their block of flats in Hackney. But, she thought, she'd never seen him hit anyone. Would Raymond provoke him to that point today?

'No one's denying that you're their father,' Dermot said loudly and firmly. 'But being someone's father carries responsibility as well as the fun parts. Being a man means setting an example, and you're not setting a good one at this minute, are you? Just look at your boy's face.'

They looked up again. Daniel attempted a feeble wave. 'I'm OK, Dad,' he said, but the wobble in his voice told them otherwise.

'I wanted to be there for them, you know?' Raymond said, a catch in his voice. 'It's not my fault things didn't turn out the right way.'

Natalia took a couple of steps forward so that she could continue to hear what was being said. The last of the spectators in the street moved away, sensing that the spectacle was largely over.

Raymond had managed to retain his dreadlocks while in prison. His skin was a very light brown, almost yellow, with darker spots of colour. His wide mouth, smiling in the photograph she'd seen in Rasheda's kitchen, had full, chiselled lips. He was the same height as Dermot, about five foot ten inches, but slightly built. Jason's impressive physique must have been inherited from his mother.

He wore a plain red, high-necked T-shirt over loose jeans, and his feet were thrust into sandals. She couldn't see a bag. Where could his belongings be? Had they just let him out this morning? And did he have any money?

'What are you wanting to achieve here?' Dermot was saying. 'Is it a bed for the night, or is it Daniel you'd like to spend time with? I think that boy is getting mixed messages here. What do you think?'

'I think you're really pissing me off with all these questions,' Raymond said, but his demeanour was quieter now. 'I spent last night in a hostel. Bloody horrible it was.'

'Listen, I know a few good places, cheap and cheerful, that you could stay in around here. The boys I look after on the construction site are always needin' a place to sleep that isn't like an old-fashioned doss house but where they can be free to come and go. I can give you some addresses if you like.'

'Maybe. But don't go offering me work. I don't do building sites.' Ray looked up. 'Hear that? I'm not doing no bloody building work. Is that why you got him round here?'

Rasheda wisely said nothing, but pulled Daniel closer to her in a hug. He immediately pulled away, embarrassed.

'When can I see my dad?' he asked, quite clearly.

'Well, I'm not offering you work, I've got

all the men I need. So that's OK.' Dermot was keeping Raymond focussed on himself. 'Have you got a mobile phone so I can contact you with the addresses?'

'OK, OK,' Raymond sighed and put his hand in his pocket. Natalia tensed. Supposing he had a knife in there? But he pulled out a mobile phone. 'It's new, I don't know the number.'

New or 'recently acquired'? she wondered and looked up at Rasheda, who met her eye and rolled hers.

Dermot made a note of the number, then said, 'What you need to do now is back right off. You're going to have to make an arrangement to meet your son, Daniel. Jason's big enough to sort things out for himself.'

'Yeah,' Raymond gave a fleeting smile. 'How did I manage to produce a policeman?' But he wasn't done with Rasheda yet. 'You can't shut me out for ever you know,' he shouted at her. 'You know we belong together.'

Rasheda shook her head. When she spoke, her voice was low and even, her words not to be denied. 'I don't think we do, not any more, Raymond. I'm sorry. I've changed. I want a different life now.'

Raymond looked quite shocked at her words. He turned to Dermot. 'I thought she was just putting on a show. You know, so that I had to fight my way back in. She can't really mean what she's just said, can she?'

'I think if you want Daniel and Rasheda in your life again, you're going to have to work at it,' Dermot said. 'What are you going to do now?'

Raymond sighed. 'Look up a few of me old mates, I suspect. No point hanging around here.'

With a final look up at Rasheda, he called, 'I'll give you a ring, son, and then we'll get together. OK?'

'OK, Dad!' Finally, Daniel smiled and waved.

Raymond turned and began to walk down the street, shoulders bowed.

'You two want to come in?' Rasheda said quietly, so Raymond wouldn't hear.

Dermot looked at Natalia, who shook her head. 'It's OK, Rasheda, Dermot and me've got things to do – and so have you. Call me later, OK?'

As she and Dermot began to walk along the road back to Stoke Newington High Street – they'd got a taxi up there for speed – she realised that some of her faith in her husband had been restored.

'You handled that really well, Dermot,' she said. 'Thank you for helping my friend out, when ... well, you know.'

'When we were having our first major row?' he said. 'I handled Raymond better than I'm handling the row, is what you mean.'

'No, I don't. I wish you'd understand.'

He halted so she did, too, and faced her. 'Natalia, it's usually men who are supposed to bottle things up. But you've been bottling something up. I was doing some thinking back there. Tell me now, this expecting to see Jem everywhere – is it because you still carry a torch for him? Your first love, the father of your child? Or is it because you fear him? I have to know. Talk to me.'

'I fear him still.' Natalia forced the words out. 'I fight it every day. I didn't want to tell you, to worry you. I didn't want you to make the mistake of thinking he still meant something to me.'

Dermot nodded. 'I'm not going to say, you should have told me. But I knew something was wrong between us, that you were holding something back. I thought maybe you felt I was trying to pressurise you in some way. I'm not.' He smiled. 'So you don't want to leave me and go back home to your mother, lovely as she is?'

'No, I don't.' Natalia smiled tremulously. 'Can we get through this? Can you forgive me for not talking to you?'

'I'll try. Hmm, yes, I think I will be able to.'

Shyly, feeling a little shaky, Natalia held out her hand. 'I'm feeling very hot and sticky. I may need another shower.'

'That's a good idea.' He took her hand. 'I think I need one, too.'

24

Natalia did not feel in a party mood, but she knew she wasn't going to have any choice in the matter – she had to join in. She was still finding it hard to believe that Donna was leaving them. Events had moved swiftly since the announcement that the department boss had achieved the promotion she was after. Barely two weeks later, she was having her leaving party, venue still to be announced, even though it was that night. And Donna had not offered an invitation, she had ordered Natalia and her colleagues to be there – albeit with a dazzling smile.

Donna's exuberance, held in check until now, had been obvious all day. Was she so glad to be leaving her old colleagues behind? Natalia watched her as she methodically cleared out the drawers of her desk, packed her big, orange bird of paradise plant in a box, which would be taken away by the removal men along with her chrome coat stand, the photograph of her father, Colonel Harris, and other personal items that had been stowed in two smaller cardboard boxes, to her new office somewhere in south London.

However, this was not a new, relaxed Donna, this was Donna buzzing with excitement and energy. Her stratagems had at last worked. She was on the next rung of her own personal ladder. Perhaps she would be a mite sad to say goodbye to her old colleagues, but the new challenge was already beckoning and taking up her full attention.

With the added bonus, of course, Natalia mused, that she would continue to be able to spend time in the company of Area Commander Jonathan Crane. So far he did not appear to have surrendered to Donna's charms – in fact he had not put in an appearance at the Lost Property Office the past two weeks. It was a relief not to have had to face him on a daily basis. But of course those meetings had largely been to set up the Disaster Management Exercise. Natalia recalled the moment when he'd laid his hand on her arm, running his fingers down to her hand, closing his fingers on hers, dark eyes intent...

She grew warm thinking about it and glanced round almost guiltily, but no one else was giving her any notice. Donna did not seem at all put out at his non-appearance. Would he be at the party tonight? Natalia wondered. And if so, how would she deal with his presence?

Natalia doubted that he would come on to her again. While there was no denying that he was an attractive man, at the same time there had been something – she hadn't yet been able to put her finger on it – underneath his chat-up lines that made her feel uneasy.

She looked across at Donna, taking yet another phone call. She'd been on the phone most of the day, in between clearing, packing, and instructing Avon, fielding calls from well-wishers.

Donna's shining, blonde hair fell loose to her shoulders. She had abandoned her trouser suit for a tight, short, black dress that displayed her shapely, muscled legs, and was wearing serious black-patent high heels that Avon had been admiring all day. She had a black bolero jacket with big buttons to slip on over her dress.

She was dressed to kill, and Jonathan Crane was her target. Would tonight be her night? Had he been waiting till she was no longer the boss of the Lost Property Office to make his move?

Donna appeared at the door of her office and beckoned to Avon. Avon stood up quickly, horn in hand, and gave a couple of sharp toots.

'I'm in Donna's office,' she announced generally and unnecessarily. Then could not resist a further toot. 'Taxis are arriving at six to take us to the party. Don't forget, be ready on time.'

Toot toot. Toot toot. Then she marched into Donna's office, still carrying her horn.

'I think it's about time that horn suffered a horrible injury,' Mark said, swinging round in his chair to face Natalia. 'All you need is a pin to slide into the bulb.'

'I think she's tooted it more times today than she did when she first got it,' Natalia said.

'I could write a bestseller, one hundred and one uses of a dead horn.'

'Only thing is, Avon might be our new boss. She would not be pleased.'

They reverted to the main topic of conversation in the office since they had learned of Donna's promotion.

Mark grimaced. 'If she is promoted, she might get a newer, bigger, shinier horn! Or several of them.'

'Seriously though, it might not be her.'

'Ranjiv's a very steady man.' They could just see the top of Ranjiv's greying head over his computer screen.

'But he wants to retire soon. Go early. He wouldn't want the responsibility. Can you imagine Cliff in Donna's office?'

Natalia smiled. 'I don't think Cliff would want to give up running the vault – and by the way, I figured out why he's been so grouchy lately. I told him smoking is bad for his health – and maybe his love life.' Fond though she was of Mark, she would not betray Cliff's attraction to Avon. 'He's been trying to give up smoking.'

'Of course! Stefan said he hardly ever saw him outside any more. We thought he was smoking in the ... you know where. Special Items Room. A post-magazine ciggy, know what I mean?'

'Mark! Enough!'

Toot toot.

'Oh no, she's back,' Natalia said. 'And here are Cliff and Stefan – oh, Cliff's closing up the vault early.' She saw that the lights had been switched off, and Cliff was beginning to pull the metal security door across prior to locking it. 'Mark, do you know where the party's going to be?'

Mark shrugged. 'Sorry Natalia. But I do know it's going to be some party. I heard Donna's put a lot of money behind the bar, wherever it is, and hired a DJ for dancing later on. Hey, mate, what's going on?' He turned away to talk to Stefan. Natalia took out her mobile phone and pressed the speed dial for Dermot's number.

'Hi, baby,' he answered straight away. 'How's it going?'

'OK.' Dermot's voice had sounded as if he was standing right next to her. Natalia felt a sudden ache to put her arms around him. Was she getting clingy all of a sudden? 'Where are you?'

'Just leaving the site now and heading home. Nuala is in charge of bringing Connor over, I'm expecting them around seven.'

As Kathleen and Nathan wanted an evening alone together to celebrate his birthday, Dermot had given up his night out with the boys and instead was spending it with his children.

'What about you?' he asked.

'Everyone's getting ready for Donna's party. She's ordered taxis for six o'clock, but I don't know where they're taking us yet.'

'From what you've told me about her, it'll be somewhere decent.'

'I suppose I have to go.'

'Of course you do. You go on and have a good time. Let your hair down.'

'But from what Mark tells me, the party might go on until late. I wish you were coming with me.' Dermot knew she still hated going to parties without him.

'Well, I couldn't let the children down now, could I? And an evening with just me and them can't be a bad idea now and then, can it?'

'You mean I'm coming between you?' Natalia asked, suddenly annoyed. 'I always try to give you space–'

'You're reading too much into what I'm saying. It's not about you at all. You're great, you know I think that. But every now and then, just me and them can't be a bad thing.'

'I suppose. All the same, I still wish you were coming tonight. I can always leave early and get a taxi home.'

'Course you can. But I bet you'll have a great time when you get there. Just relax and enjoy yourself. You might be surprised.'

Natalia glared at the phone when she rang off. He'd said he had no intention of pressurising her any more to start their own family, but hadn't that been just what he was doing? Painting a rosy picture of the strength of his ties with his children. Children of his own blood. Who had inherited his hair, his eyes. And he had a son who bore his name. Those special ties were something he and Natalia did not share. Yet.

Or had he really meant what he said: go and have a good time.

'Natalia?' A quiet voice beside her broke into her unhappy thoughts. It was Rose. 'I've switched my computer off now. Shall we go to the ladies and get ready for the party? I've bought a new dress to wear, I'd like to have your opinion on it. Or I could go like this.'

Natalia looked up. Rose was wearing a white T-shirt and a long, blue skirt decorated with small, white flowers over her narrow slim frame. Around her neck, as always, was the small, gold cross on a chain.

'Have you had highlights done?' Natalia asked, seeing a subtle lighter shade in her brown hair.

Rose nodded.

'They look so good on you, I just had a few, not too bright.' Involuntarily, they both glanced over at Avon's bright-red hair with fiery sunset streaks, standing out from her head in carefully sculpted spikes and layers.

'I'm dying to see your dress.' Natalia said, standing up and gladly switching off her computer. 'It's impossible to do any more work. You'd think we were all going on holiday.'

Rose smiled. 'Donna was very good at keeping us all working hard without realising what a tight control she had on us.'

'You'll miss her.'

Rose nodded. 'She was a very fair boss.'

'And you don't know who you'll be working for next?'

They continued their speculation about the future of the department as they went upstairs to the more spacious and comfortable ladies beside the conference rooms. Rose changed into her dress and looked shyly at Natalia as she came out of the cubicle. The dress she'd chosen was pale-blue, fitted, with a round neckline not low enough to reveal any cleavage, and she wore a wide belt that emphasised her slenderness. Natalia noticed she wore clear nail varnish, too.

'You look lovely,' she confirmed. 'Stefan's a lucky man.'

Rose looked up sharply, 'Stefan? What has he been saying? I told him I had yet to make up my mind about whether to date him or not.'

Natalia shook her head. 'Rose, Stefan has said nothing to me. But he is a good man. If you like him, don't hold back because of the exterior he puts on here. There's more to him than all that bravado.'

'I know,' Rose murmured. 'We attend the same church, you see. I was surprised to see him there at first. But the more time I spend with him, the more I see a different side to him. I just don't know which one to trust.'

'All you can do is trust your own heart, Rose.'

Rose smiled shyly at Natalia while Natalia put on some pale-blue eye shadow, black mascara, and pale-pink lipstick, as well as touching up her make-up. Now she put on a necklace, a big, pale-pink round shell on a ribbon tie. She was wearing a pale-pink dress with a matching pink shrug and she'd had her nails done in pink, too. The two women examined themselves in the mirror.

'One pink, one blue,' Rose commented. 'I think we'll do.'

Natalia tried to fluff up her hair a bit but it fell, fine and flat, to her shoulders. 'We'll have to do,' she said. 'Let's go on down.'

When they re-entered the office, Natalia saw that not only had everyone stopped working and were now standing around chatting, but that Jason had arrived, with Detective Sergeant Jack Riley. She was relieved to see there was no sign of Jonathan Crane. Jack was talking to Stefan and Donna outside her office. Natalia went over to Jason, who was looking Rose up and down admiringly as she went to join the younger contingent of Mark, Stefan and Ranjit.

'I haven't noticed her before,' Jason said, nudging Jack. 'Is she new?'

'No, but her dress is.' Natalia gave a thumbs-up to Rose in her head. 'You're not in uniform tonight. Joining the party?'

'Donna invited Jack and me, as we'll be working closely together in the future, she said.'

'What about your mum?'

Jason shook his head. 'I've got a message from her for you. She sends her love, but says she won't be coming. She's supervising a meeting between Daniel and our dad. Basically, they're all going out for a pizza together.'

Disappointed though she was not to have Rasheda's company tonight, Natalia was relieved for her friend that she'd been able to arrange a friendly meeting.

'How do you feel about that? Have you seen Raymond?'

'We went for a drink together the other night. But he wasn't happy. Said I was dissing him.'

'Why's that?'

'I told him never to give my mum grief like that again or he'd have me to deal with. Thanks to Dermot, it came out OK this time. But if I'd been there–' Jason bunched a fist.

Natalia nodded. Rasheda had made a wise move in not calling Jason. 'Is Honey joining us later?'

'Nah, she's out with a friend of hers. Gone to see a girly movie together.'

'Right, everyone, taxi'll be here soon!' Donna's voice could be heard above the general hubbub. 'Gather round, I just want to say a few words.'

'While you're still sober!' a cheeky voice ventured.

Donna flashed a grin as they all clustered around the entrance to her office. While she gave a small speech saying how much she'd enjoyed working with them, how she hoped they'd stay in touch, Mark sidled up to Natalia and whispered, 'Who's got the leaving present?'

'Stefan. He's hidden it in reception. We'll pick it up when we go,' she whispered back. They'd collected enough to buy Donna a new set of running shoes.

'What's this?' Cliff said, as the smattering of applause died away at the end of Donna's short speech. 'A parcel for you, Donna.' He'd perched his bottom on the edge of Rose's desk, disturbing some papers to reveal a small, padded bag.

'I'm sorry, Donna,' Rose said. 'I didn't see that before.'

'No harm done,' Donna said, picking it up and looking at the typed label.

'Aren't you going to open it?' Avon said, eyes gleaming avidly behind her glasses.

'All right then,' Donna said, tearing it open and putting her hand inside. Everyone's eyes were on her as she drew out a very flimsy pair of black knickers. She held them up. They were nothing more than a thong with a small triangle of black silk at the front decorated with a feathery fringe.

'That's a bit near the knuckle,' Avon said, disappointed. 'Bloomin' cheek if you ask me.'

'That's a good one, cheek, cheeks, geddit?' Mark was irrepressible as ever.

'Donna has secret admirer,' Stefan said.

'Not the only one around here,' Avon remarked, staring at Rose.

Donna smiled mysteriously, but made no comment. She tucked them back into the padded bag they'd come in, and said, 'Are we all ready?'

'Just one more thing.' Stefan stepped forward, bringing from behind his back a plastic box. 'For you, Rose,' he said, handing it to her and looking challengingly at Avon. 'I am no longer secret admirer.'

Rose opened the box and took out a white orchid corsage, which he pinned to her blue dress, while she murmured her thanks. So it was just as Natalia had thought. Stefan had been the one courting Rose with flowers and chocolates. It was for Stefan that Rose had really blossomed tonight.

What would Avon say? She was staring

blankly, disbelievingly, at the orchid corsage on Rose's shoulder.

'All very nice,' Donna said briskly. 'I've just had a text – taxis are here!'

They all began moving towards the exit. Natalia hung back, to help Stefan pick up Donna's leaving present and the card they'd all signed.

'Should I congratulate you, Stefan? Have you won Rose's heart at last?' she said softly.

He smiled. 'At least she's letting me try now.'

'You've been plying her with gifts for some time, haven't you? I realised it had to be you when she mentioned she went to St Stephen's Church in West Hampstead, not far from you.'

He nodded. 'We attend the same Roman Catholic church and at first we just talked as friends in the congregation there until one day I realised–'

'That she is the one?'

'Yes. I'm sure of it. Her soul fits mine. Now I must make her believe it, too.'

'I think Avon will take it badly.'

'Tch, that woman persuaded herself the only reason I took her hooter and sent the emails was because I fancied her. She could not accept that I was not interested and still

277

carried on stalking me. Perhaps now she will forget me.'

Perhaps now Cliff might have a chance with Avon, if he decided to make his move.

Half an hour later, drawing up outside the pub, Natalia recognised the bar as soon as she stepped out of the taxi. It was your typical Victorian London pub, with dark, red-and-green ceramic tiles lining part of the outside walls. Hanging baskets spilled bright trails of busy lizzies, petunias and fuchsias above punter's heads outside. Situated on the corner off a small cul de sac and the main Camden High Street drag. *The Glass and Bottle*.

Natalia looked anxiously towards Rose and Donna and Avon. A Friday night, she knew this was the night Fred had targeted his victims. Surely, she was being paranoid though. She'd allowed her imagination to carry her away once before here, with Dave and Mel. She had to let this go. Everything was going to be fine. This was a party. She needed to let her hair down and relax.

25

Inside, the pub was filled with balloons, streamers, and a big banner proclaiming 'Good Luck, Donna'. Someone had gone to a great deal of effort to decorate the room for the party.

'Wow, guys, this is great,' Donna said, gazing around. 'Who dreamed this up?'

Avon stepped forward. 'I couldn't let you go without the best send off,' she said, puffing up with pride and delight that she'd pleased the woman she admired so much.

There was something different about her, Natalia thought. She wasn't wearing her glasses. Was she trying out contact lenses? Was that for Stefan's benefit, an attempt to win him away from Rose?

'It's brilliant, Avon, thanks,' said Donna. 'OK, everyone, let's party!'

'Watch out – let me get that balloon out of your way.' Jack Riley's concerned voice sounded at Natalia's shoulder, just as a balloon landed on her head, its trailing ribbons threatening to get entangled in her hair.

Laughing, Natalia bent forward so that he could grab hold of the balloon and then bat it on its way.

'Mark's got quite a game going on down the other end of the bar,' Jack said. 'Who can bat a balloon furthest.'

'That one must be the winner,' Natalia said. 'Whose was that?'

'I think it was Cliff's – oh, your glass is empty. Want another one? I'm just getting a beer for myself.'

'Thanks, I'll have a white wine.'

Jack waved to catch the attention of one of the young bartenders, and she came to take his order, while Natalia looked around.

As well as Natalia's immediate work colleagues at the Lost Property Office, Donna had invited back-room administrative staff, officials from TFL, and other members of the Transport Police, and soon the bar was packed. Bar staff were kept at full stretch serving every kind of drink from soft drinks to beers, from wine to spirits and cocktails.

Stefan and Rose sat together on a leather sofa, Mark and Jason opposite. Stefan sat watching Rose as if he couldn't quite believe she was real and at his side. No wonder he'd been moody, Natalia thought, falling in love with someone as strong minded as quiet

Rose was, and keeping it hidden from his work colleagues.

'Here's your wine, Natalia.' Jack smiled. He wasn't bad looking, Natalia thought. He might not have that edge of danger that Jonathan Crane exuded, but that made her feel safe and more relaxed. Then he frowned. 'I don't know about you, but I think it's nicer to have a partner with you at an event like this. Someone to share it with.'

'True. My husband is looking after his children tonight.' She didn't add 'or he would be here' because she wasn't sure Dermot would've come anyway. Were their differences becoming insurmountable?

'Of course, you're a married woman. I think that's why I find it easy to talk to you. So many women today are career oriented, like to take charge. I'm not sure I know how to handle them. Maybe that's why I'm on my own tonight.'

Was that why things hadn't worked between him and Donna?

'I think a career woman would be glad of a man to take charge sometimes,' Natalia advised. 'It gives them a break. As long as he wasn't a control freak.'

'Oh no, of course. But there are so many women out there without anyone to take care of them these days. Living alone, vulnerable. It's not right, is it?'

Natalia thought of Polly sitting alone in her garden drinking wine and reading romantic novels. 'I don't know about right,' she said cautiously. 'Living alone doesn't always mean someone is lonely.'

Jack sighed and sipped his beer. 'And sometimes it does. Any other tips for the lonely bachelor?'

Natalia picked up her wine and drank.

'You're good at talking to women,' she started, but in the next moment Donna lurched up to them. 'What's all this serious talk in the corner?' she said. 'Get ready for the DJ. He's great. He's really hot.'

'Really? How'd you find him?' Jack's expression had brightened up.

'Fantastic party I went to a little while ago in the country.'

'You'll have to have a dance with me,' Jack said.

'You bet. Show you some moves.'

'I've got some moves of my own,' he smiled broadly.

'Really. Well, you've been keeping them a secret from me. When are you going to show me?'

As the flirting continued, Natalia murmured, 'Excuse me,' and edged away.

Engrossed with each other, they didn't notice her go. Was this going to be Donna's lucky night in more ways than one? Were those saucy knickers a gift from Jack, after all? If so, he'd managed to stay very cool when she'd opened the package. But Donna had looked as if she knew exactly who they were from.

Joining Stefan and Mark, Natalia found the conversation flowed easily between them. Then Mark persuaded her to referee him and Jason in a lively debate about European football, even though she protested she wasn't an expert on football teams, not even Polish ones. Donna meanwhile was flitting from group to group and really letting her hair down, drinking wine freely. Then food was brought in to a side table and everyone tucked in. Natalia realised she was a little tipsy and was glad of the food to soak up the booze. You told me to have a good time, Dermot, she thought, so I will, and if I don't get home early, then don't start complaining to me!

Right on cue the DJ, BBZee, came to the microphone and went into his patter. She recognised his accent as a Newcastle one, from the presenters she'd seen on television.

He wore a loose cotton shirt with a stand-up collar and the sleeves torn off, two necklaces round his throat of seashells threaded on bootlaces, various wristlets including Save the Planet and Feed the World. His jeans were modelled on the Boss, Bruce Springsteen, rather than Eminem. When he yelled, 'Are you ready?' Natalia found herself joining in the resounding 'Yes!' as the energy level in the packed bar went up several notches.

Flashing lights strobed across the small dance floor in front of the BBZee's set-up and speakers, and first on the floor was Avon, strutting her stuff, quickly joined by a couple of lads Natalia recognised as experts in fire control; Transport Police from the disaster exercise they'd taken part in.

Cliff stood by himself, watching morosely. Natalia went over to him and although he didn't look at her, his eyes glued to Avon's gyrating form, he growled, 'I'd do anything for a cigarette.'

'How are you getting on?'

'I've gone seven days now without one, but I'm usin' up the nicotine patches very fast.'

'That's fantastic, Cliff It's not going to be easy when you've smoked all your life. And if you do give in and have one, try not to give up and start smoking again.'

'That's all very well, but it'd be easier if I felt it was all worthwhile.' He glowered at the dance floor as Avon followed the instructions to 'shake your booty' to the letter, to whoops and claps from the young lads around her.

'It's worth it for your health,' Natalia declared, finding it hard to keep still. The music was getting to her and she wanted to dance, but by herself? Without Dermot? She quickly swallowed the rest of her wine, and felt her head spin. What was Cliff saying?

'Och, even if she gives up on Stefan at last, she'll never give me a second look.'

So he'd been aware of Avon's unrequited crush on Stefan all this while. BBZee was still catering for all generations at the party, and put on a Rolling Stones classic. No doubt later on, when only the young ones were left, he'd be playing a very different kind of music.

She grabbed Cliff's elbow. 'Come. Dance with me.'

'Me! You're kidding. I don't dance.'

'I don't care. I want to dance and I don't want to dance alone. Just stand in front of me. Please, Cliff.'

He sighed loudly. 'Only for you, Natalia,' and allowed her to lead him over to the dance floor.

For the moment, Natalia gave herself up to the music, letting the beat carry her away. Cliff did as she'd asked and stood with her, swaying slightly, trying not to look pained. Then the Stones faded to be replaced by, in BBZee's words, 'Everyone's disco fave – it was cool to hate them, now it's cool to love them – Abba!'

To her surprise, Cliff did not make a bee-line off the floor. Instead, his face lit up and he began to move more energetically, using his arms as well. He looked OK. Avon was still dancing and she bumped into Cliff from behind. She laughed and patted his bottom – then stared in shock as he turned around and she realised who it was. Cliff's face was transformed by a smile.

'See,' she mouthed. 'There's hope!'

The Abba mix ended and Natalia thanked Cliff and left the dance floor. She made her way over towards the door, where it was quieter and cooler, and fanned herself. Romance was in the air, she thought. Stefan and Rose were still very much together, chatting to Mark and Jason. And who knew, a night on the dance floor just might bring those two opposites, Avon and Cliff, together.

As for Donna and Jack, where had they got to? She looked through the chattering crowds, the volume of noise having gone up since the music started. Was that Donna's blonde head just there? Natalia felt a cool breeze at her back and turned round. A new guest was arriving at the party. It was Jonathan Crane! And, she had to admit, he looked good in his party clothes. He too was wearing jeans, but figure-hugging, outlining his strong thigh muscles. He wore a white, collarless shirt tucked into his jeans, emphasising his tan and his dark colouring. But when his eyes lighted on her, she felt again that strange sense of unease she always found in his company.

'Natalia,' he said. 'Looking good tonight.' He smiled. Like a predator, she thought. He gave the bar a quick, searching scan. 'Looks like I've got some catching up to do. I've only just now escaped from work. Good thing I only live around the corner. Quick shower and I was here.'

'You help yourself at the bar to whatever you want to drink. Donna's paying,' Natalia said. 'But I don't think there's any food left.'

'I'm not after food,' he said, again with

that predatory smile.

When he saw the look on her face, he quickly became conciliatory. 'Seriously, can I buy you a drink, Natalia? Make amends for the other day.'

'Sure,' Natalia answered, not wanting to be seen to be holding a grudge, or any bad feeling.

'Jon! Jonathan! I thought you weren't going to make it.' Donna brushed past Natalia, staggering on her black-patent high heels, then put her arms round Jonathan and kissed him on both cheeks.

'As I said, looks like I've got some catching up to do on you lot,' he said.

Had Donna overstepped the mark, Natalia wondered. How would her new boss react? Jonathan gave her a couple of air kisses back. He did not pull away, but neither did he wrap his arms around her in return. Or was that just because he was aware they were on public show.

'Well, you'd better get started,' Donna said, grinning tipsily and keeping one arm around him. 'Because I'm way ahead of you, and I want you to catch up, so that I can thank you properly. Know what I mean?'

'Not sure that I do. There's no need to thank me for the promotion, I was just one voice on the board.'

Donna flung back her head and laughed uproariously. 'You're so funny. I don't mean the job, you ninny.' She leaned into him and whispered in his ear. Natalia realised that this conversation wasn't meant for her, and turned away, meaning to go and join Mark, but she heard Jonathan say, 'Knickers? What knickers?' and Donna reply quite loudly, 'Don't be so coy. I know they were from you.'

'I'm sorry, Donna, you've got some other secret admirer. They're not from me.' Jonathan's tone was not unfriendly, but there was no mistaking from its firmness that he was speaking the truth.

'Oh, God, I feel such an idiot!'

Donna lurched past Natalia, pushing her quite hard in the back. Natalia caught a glimpse of her face, red with embarrassment and heard her mutter, 'I'm getting these ridiculous knickers off, they're killing me,' and then she was making a beeline for the ladies.

The greasy saxophone of Jerry Rafferty's 'Baker Street Blues' blasting out from the pub's sound system distracted Natalia from the drama of the Donna, Jonathan and Jack triangle. Dermot loved this track. He'll be sorry he missed it, she thought, gazing into space. The last time they'd listened to this together had been that time they'd gone out between Christmas and New Year, exploring unknown parts of London on their days off, and they'd found a great, old-fashioned pub with good food and an even better jukebox.

'Are you all right, Natalia?' Rose's soft voice broke into her thoughts. 'You looked miles away.'

'Thank you, I am fine. Fantastic even.' She smiled. 'I must ring my husband.'

She headed for the door, ready to step outside if she couldn't hear Dermot's voice properly. 'What? Who is it?' Dermot's sleepy voice answered.

'It's your wife calling. Who else were you expecting?'

'Ah, Angelina Jolie turned me down again, so you'll do. What's up, are you leaving now?'

'Soon. Listen to me, Mr O'Shea, I love you. I love you very much.'

'I hear you, Mrs O'Shea, and for you to ring me up in the middle of a party to tell me that I'll be guessing you've had a drink. Or two. Or three. Are you pissed already?'

'Do I have to be pissed to realise how

much you mean to me and to tell you how stupid I've been?'

'Uh oh, what have you done?'

'Nothing! I've been thinking about what *we* are going to be doing.'

'Our holiday in September? Funny time to be thinking about a second honeymoon.'

'Or even before our holiday. I've been thinking about having our baby together.'

'Natalia, I'm keeping my promise. The pressures off in that department. If you want to wait until you've found Paul, then I will wait.'

'I don't want to wait any longer. Time is rushing on, and I'm tired of living in the past. What you said earlier, about the special bond with your own children, of your own blood. That's something I want to share with you. I will make sure that Paul knows my love for him has never wavered or lessened, whether there is a new baby or not. Nuala and Connor, too, you'll have to go through the same argument with them.'

'I don't know what to say ... it's the last thing I was expectin' ... oh, Natalia it's going to be wonderful. I'm a lucky man, so I am.'

'We're both lucky. Love is fragile, and if you're lucky enough to have it well, just think of all those people who don't have it, or who haven't made it when they do have it.' She thought of Cliff and Avon, Donna and her thing for policemen – and then Stefan's fight for Rose. 'I'm going to get a taxi home very soon.'

'When you're ready, love. I'll be waiting.'

She rang off and headed back into the partying throng. She would thank Donna for a great party, and say goodnight.

'Hi, Natalia, have you seen Rose?' It was Stefan. 'I've got us a cab waiting outside. We leave now. You want to share taxi, Natalia?'

'Thanks, but we live in opposite directions – I'll be all right. And I want to say goodbye to Donna first'

'Could you look in ladies for Rose? She say she only be a minute. That ten minutes ago.'

'Sure, Stefan. I'll go look. You seen Donna?'

'We don't find her yet. We are looking, too.'

One or two other people, bags over their shoulders, light jackets on and ready to leave, were also looking around for Donna. Natalia walked over to the bar, where the manager was checking one of the tills.

'Excuse me. Have you seen Donna Harris? The woman who hired this bar from you?'

'Oh, yes, Donna.' He was young, dressed in a smart suit with a wide, green tie. 'Last I saw she was heading out to the ladies. I remember 'cos I asked how long she wanted the till to stay open and she said, till the last one leaves.'

'Thanks.' Natalia hurried to the end of the bar, past the pulsating dance floor, turned left then found the door marked 'Toilets'. She pushed through it and found herself in the narrow corridor painted cream with a floor of small, red tiles. Still part of the original old building, she thought. A hand-painted sign in black on the wall said 'Toilets this way' with an arrow pointing to the right. She followed it and found first the door marked 'Gents' and then the one marked 'Ladies'. She glanced around it and saw the old-fashioned door, also painted black, with a brass doorknob and two bolts on it, both open. It was the 'Exit' she and Polly had pushed their way through the other week.

Just then, the gents opened and Natalia pressed herself up against the wall, only it wasn't a man who stepped out but the cleaner from the other day.

'Eh, it's you. Was just thinking about you.'

'You were?' Natalia questioned, thinking that was odd.

'Yeah, pretty certain I saw yer fella here. The guy who helped yer girl out the other day. What was his name again? Freddy?'

'Fred? Fred was here?'

Natalia's hand raced to her throat.

'All I know was it was a dead cert for the fella who carried your friend out.'

My God, it was Friday night. It was midnight. And Mornington Crescent tube station was just a stone's throw away.

Fred had been there.

'What did he look like?' Natalia interrogated, grabbing the cleaner by the arm.

'Medium height. Brown hair. Black shirt. Good-looking. Ach, I don't know,' she exclaimed, shrugging Natalia's arm off. 'But I'd recognise him again.'

Racing to the ladies toilets, Natalia pushed the door open, praying that Donna and Rose were enjoying a girlie goodbye moment, and that was why Rose had been absent so long.

Inside, out of the four cubicles, two doors were shut, and it was in the typical state of a pub toilet at the end of a boozy evening. Loo paper lay about on the floor, having been used as hand towel and then dropped.

294

In one case, a trail of it led back into the cubicle. The surface around the washbasins was pooled with water. Natalia banged on each cubicle.

'Donna?'

No answer.

'Rose?'

Pressing at the door, she could tell it was locked from the inside. Getting onto her hands and knees, she looked under the door. The first thing she saw was a pink shell necklace lying on the ground.

'Natalia, is that you?'

Suddenly, the cubicle door opened and out stepped Rose, dabbing tissue paper to her mouth, the necklace clutched in her hand.

'Didn't feel too well,' Rose explained. 'Must have been something I ate. Well, it certainly wasn't anything I drank.'

Dimly, Natalia recalled that Rose was a teetotaller.

When Rose saw the look on Natalia's face though, she dropped her hand to her side.

'Have you seen Donna, Rose?'

'No, no, I haven't. Whatever's wrong, Natalia?'

Please, God, Natalia prayed, let Donna have gone back inside and the manager not have noticed. Let her be in a corner somewhere with Jonathan, Natalia wished, as she hurried out into the corridor and back into the bar.

Spotting Jason, she called out, 'Oh, Jason. Where's the Area Commander?'

Find him and she'd find Donna, she reckoned.

Jason paused, bottle of lager at his lips. He glanced around. 'Sorry, Natalia. I don't see him. Someone said he was going home, he just stopped by for a bit.'

Going home? Yes, of course, he lived nearby. But she'd been beside the door for some time. He hadn't left that way. A niggle of anxiety formed in her mind.

Avon was standing at the edge of the dance floor. She'd discarded her see-through over shirt and wore a sun top with skimpy straps over a short skirt. Her face was red and shining with perspiration. Cliff was nowhere to be seen.

Natalia went up to her. 'Have you seen Donna?' she asked.

Avon shook her head. 'Not for ages. Why?'

Natalia didn't want to panic anyone unnecessarily. There was still a chance Donna had gone back with the Area Commander. 'Several of us wanted to thank her and say goodnight but ... no one's seen her for quite a while.'

'I saw her.' One of the lads Avon had been dancing with overheard her. 'I was just coming out of the gents when I saw her in the corridor outside.' He giggled. 'She was really out of it, dead drunk. Her feller was helping her out the back door for some fresh air.'

'Did you get a look at him?' Natalia demanded, grabbing at his arm.

'Nah. Too dark, weren't it?'

Natalia felt a shiver run down her spine.

'Avon, who chose this venue?' she asked.

'Donna did. Jonathan lives nearby, she said. I might get lucky. Maybe she has.'

'Or maybe she's been very unlucky,' Natalia muttered.

26

Natalia heard her footsteps echoing as she headed at top speed for the traffic island and the statue of Cobden. Although it had been a bright day and was still dry, it was cooler than of late and there were fewer passers-by at this hour than she and Polly had encountered several weeks ago. The lights were against her and, on the corner beside Koko, she fretted until she was able to run across the road.

Of course there was a possibility that Jonathan had simply taken Donna back home to his place, but out of the back way so that his work colleagues wouldn't see him. Only she couldn't take that chance. Fred had been in the pub. Fred could be someone she knew. Thoughts and questions that had been turning over in her mind for weeks now began to tumble into place.

Which way would he have taken her in this time? Would he have used the cleaner's entrance, secure in the knowledge that they would be upstairs and he could roam freely through the office floor before descending. Or would he use the main entrance?

Natalia did not have a choice. She had to run round and go in the main entrance, praying that it had not been locked for the night. The traffic moving along the Hampstead Road was well lit, and there were few people about, most people preferring to head to Camden Town station instead.

Natalia was scared. Fred had taken a huge risk this evening. If it *was* someone they knew, would he want to cover his tracks?

He'd broken his own rules now. He was on dangerous territory.

The big, metal security door was pulled part the way across, but Natalia was in time to enter. No members of staff were visible as she pressed her Oyster card on its pad and the automatic gates opened in front of her. Which way to go to reach platform level? Instinctively, she was drawn to the stairs, but she darted a glance round the corner to her left at the lifts. The red indicator lights showed that all the lifts were at street level. She followed her instinct and headed for the 66 steps to the platforms. On her right was the plate-glass window into the station-master's office. One person wearing a dark-blue shirt was in there, but he had his back to her. There was no time to stop. Natalia began to race down the stairs.

Her footsteps rang out on the stone steps. They curved downwards, and she could not see what was around the next bend. Would she come across them, still on their way down? Her heart hammering, she paused for a moment. Had she heard a sound, a cry from far below? But all she could hear was the sound of her own ragged breathing and the blood pulsing through her ears.

She grabbed hold of the handrail as she

continued her breakneck dizzying descent, her footsteps echoing hollowly. No one else was about. Had the last stopping train passed through the station yet? And even if there were a remaining few stragglers, who would look twice at a man supporting his wife or girlfriend home at this time of night after a good time in the pub or restaurant?

How much further now? And then, suddenly, a distant horn sounded, and she was plunged into darkness. If she hadn't been holding the handrail she would have stumbled and fallen. She could hear her heart thumping in her chest, hear her rasping gasps for breath.

And then the emergency lighting came on. The darkness had lasted only a matter of seconds, but those dark pictures in her mind, which had lived there for six years, were as vivid as the first day they'd formed.

She must concentrate on the here and now, though, not the echoes from her past, she told herself, and began leaping down two steps at a time. She must be near the bottom. But she knew that now the CCTV cameras had been switched off, and the electricians were at work far into the tunnel. Najjah, if it was her night on shift, and the cleaning team would be working their way down to ground level.

At last, Natalia reached the bottom of the stairs and ran onto the platform, knowing exactly where she was heading. And then she saw it. Donna's black bolero jacket lying on the stone floor, trampled and dusty. Confirmation that her fears were correct. Although she already knew the worst, before she had left the bar.

Now, in the eerie, blue glow of the emergency lights, the only sound was ghostly, far-off rumblings down the railway lines, and the click of her shoes on the platform. Shortly, she came to the cross passage where the Emergency Door was situated. Taking a deep breath, she turned into it and looked through the small window in the door.

They were on the first small landing. The man and his victim. The black-shirted figure of a man's outline, hands at the belt of his trousers, looking down at the crumpled figure of Donna lying at his feet. Her dress had ridden up over her thighs and her legs dangled at an awkward angle down the steps towards to the door, the black-patent high heels still somehow incongruously clinging to her feet.

As Natalia stared aghast, Donna raised her head from the floor and her eyes opened, but her eyes were rolling up and she couldn't focus. Her head fell back on the floor, her silken blonde hair splayed out. Natalia could see bruises forming on her arms.

Natalia looked back at the figure in the dim light. He had his back turned to her, but his head was moving. What was he saying? Were they twisted words of hate and abuse for women? Had his words lodged in the unconscious minds of his victims, erasing their confidence, undermining their belief in themselves?

Natalia grabbed hold of the door's safety handle, impotently pushing at it, and started thumping at the thickened glass in the window. Somehow she had to stop him.

'Get away from her,' she screamed.

The man turned, and Natalia pulled back, biting down on her fist.

'You? It was you.'

27

Of course, she thought, he fitted the profile as much as Jonathan did. Both had the warrant cards and swipe cards and inside information that could give them access to wherever they wanted to go on the London Underground system. And neither had been seen at the party for some time. Thinking back, Natalia was pretty sure that PDA, if she asked Cliff, would have been found at Mornington Crescent.

Detective Sergeant Jack Riley.

Jack looked up. He'd heard her. He stared at her, his brown eyes hard, his brows drawn down over them. His lips wore a thin smile and droplets of sweat beaded his forehead. More than anything else, though, what struck her was the triumphant expression he wore. But at the sight of her, Natalia, his expression turned to one of rage. Involuntarily, she took a step back, as if he were about to reach through the door and grab her by the throat. Then she stepped forward and redoubled her efforts, banging at the window and rattling at the handle.

'Stop!' she was shouting. 'Leave her alone!' If she could at least frighten him off–

Someone took hold of her arm, was pulling her away from her frenzied attack upon the door. It was Stefan.

'I must stop him,' Natalia cried, arms still flailing.

'Jason's here,' Mark said, coming up beside Stefan and holding her other arm. 'He'll sort it out.'

Grim-faced Jason stepped past them and looked through the window in the safety door. 'You bastard,' she heard him mutter. 'I trusted you.'

In the next instant, he'd taken his swipe card from his pocket, and then was releasing the door. Natalia pulled forward. She saw that Jack had started to drag Donna up the stairs. All she could see were her ankles and feet shod in the black-patent high heels. Jason leapt round Donna's prone body and with a roar launched himself on Jack. There was the sound of a scuffle and then the two men came into view, Jason trying to get an arm lock on to the detective sergeant. He had the advantage of youth and regular fitness training, but Jack had the advantage of wiliness learned over the years, and greater weight. She saw him press his hand into Jason's face and Jason's head snap back to avoid his gouging fingers. Miraculously, as the two men wrestled and tottered on the steps, they avoided treading on Donna.

'He needs help,' Mark said, and sprinted inside, closely followed by Stefan. Although Jack fought with hands, feet, and all his strength, using every dirty trick he'd learned over his years of service, he could not defeat the three young men. All four men panting, the struggle at last ended. Jason had Jack in an arm lock, Mark and Stefan either side, ready to grab him should he try to escape again.

Natalia stood in the doorway. Jack stared at her defiantly, while Jason read him his rights. His voice rang out clearly, but Natalia detected a slight tremor in his voice here and there, and she suspected his eyes would not be entirely dry. This would be a terrible shock to him. He had admired and looked up to Jack as his mentor.

Natalia squeezed past them and went to Donna. Her eyes were closed and she was trying to speak, but nothing she said made any sense. Gently, Natalia began to lift her up. She was a dead weight, still drugged. Mark came to help her, while Jason and

Stefan manhandled Jack through onto the platform.

'Thank God you came,' she said to Mark, as carefully they supported Donna into an upright position and draped an arm of hers round each of their shoulders, then began to head for the platform, her legs making ineffectual attempts at trying to walk.

'After we saw you dash out the way you did, Rose came over to Stefan saying that Donna was missing. We knew then something was wrong. So we legged it to the station.'

'Did you see the blackout?'

'We was just inside. This geezer was closing the gates when we run up, he says you've missed the last train, so Jason flashed his warrant card and he let us in. Then there was the blackout, and the gates didn't work no more so we just jumped them.' He flashed her a smile, all the time his familiar voice calming and steadying her. 'I've always wanted to do that. Then we had to run down them stairs. Jason remembered you saying before you knew where the attacks were happening.'

As they gratefully laid their burden on one of the wooden benches, Stefan was saying, 'I go now. I must check Rose is OK.'

'I ain't got my walkie talkie for down in the

tunnels,' Jason explained. 'Come and watch this piece of shit with me, Mark.'

'The cleaners are upstairs,' Natalia called out to Stefan. 'They'll be having their break in the back offices.'

Stefan nodded and then was loping down the platform, his long strides carrying him towards the stairs.

With Jack sat restrained on a bench between Mark and Jason, Natalia felt his hard eyes on her.

'This should have been the perfect night,' Jack spoke up, shaking his head. 'I told Donna Jonathan lived nearby. I knew she wouldn't be able to resist booking her party in the same neck of the woods. But I knew Jonathan didn't want her. Not enough of a challenge for him. Anyway, it was me she wanted. I'd already got her worked up with the knickers. I had to take care of her. This was her idea of foreplay. Oh yes, she needed me to take care of her all right. You can't say I've done anything wrong. It's what she wanted. I know how to please a woman.' Then he gave a weird kind of laugh.

'Yeah and what about these drugs I took from your pocket?' Jason challenged. 'Rohypnol. Mark and Stefan are witnesses and when the medics get hold of her blood, everyone'll know you have to drug women to get your jollies. They won't look twice at you otherwise.'

Natalia was glad of the distance between her and Jack. The two young men were keeping careful watch over him. Natalia managed to prop Donna up with her back against the tiled wall. She no longer had her evening bag. So she opened her own and took out her comb, carefully combing Donna's hair into place, tweaking her dress back into position, checking her over for cuts and bruises. At one point, Donna's eyes opened and she came to.

'What the hell?' she said indistinctly. 'Where am I?'

'You're safe,' Natalia told her. 'The police will be here soon.'

Donna started to laugh strangely and Natalia realised it was hysteria, but then fortunately for her she passed out again.

As she tended to Donna, Jack suddenly leapt up and tried to make a dash for it. He'd lulled Jason and Mark into a false sense of security, and Jason was left teetering on the edge of the platform, only just managing to save himself from falling on the rails.

Mark scrambled up and ran after Jack,

then leapt forward in a flying tackle, wrapped his arms around Jack's legs and brought both of them crashing to the ground. Natalia winced. They got hold of Jack again, Jason removing his belt and using it to hobble his colleague's ankles together. Then he fetched a fire hydrant from the wall and gave it to Mark.

'If he moves, use that on him,' he said. Natalia wasn't sure whether he meant use the spray or hit him with it. Then he came and stood in front of her where they could talk but he could still keep an eye on Jack.

'I'm sorry, Natalia, you were right all along,' he said.

'I knew it had to be someone with inside knowledge,' she told him. 'Someone who could use their swipe card to gain access to the station out of hours. I expect you'll find that he carried out an investigation here once, so he knows all the layout of the back rooms. That's how he gets in. He uses the back entrance into the administrative offices and sneaks his victims down the back stairs into the forbidden zone.'

'So he was already inside that tunnel, he didn't come in from the platform?'

'That's right. A friend of your mum's told me all about the back stairs. She's the one who found the women's items in there and handed them in to Lost Property.'

'And then he used his PDA to get their addresses? What was that for?'

'That's what I think. He always chose women who lived alone, who were vulnerable in some way. That's why he didn't go for Donna before. But she told us at the training exercise that she was buying a place by herself, having shared a flat before. You know how he comes across as charming and friendly, non-threatening, unlike his boss. Then, once he has assaulted a woman, he takes her home, after checking out where they live, most likely through their Oyster cards.'

'Why'd he take them to their homes?'

Natalia shook her head. 'You'll find out what his motivation was when you interview him, but my guess is that way they might think they had consensual sex with a stranger when drunk and not report an assault. And it would be a great thrill, wouldn't it, to walk up to their front doors, bold as brass, and nobody able to catch him. It's like doing it here, in Mornington Crescent station. There are cleaners about, he could've been stumbled across – it made it all the more exciting.'

'Where's the excitement in that? It makes me feel sick,' Jason commented, casting a glance up the platform at Jack, who was sitting hunched over. They could hear the clatter of feet on the stairs. Stefan had brought help. Donna stirred and moaned, her eyelids fluttered, but she did not come to.

'And I think he had some strange idea of chivalry, too,' Natalia continued. 'He seems to think he's doing these woman some kind of favour. He's probably made up a complete fantasy, which he re-enacts over and over again. Then in his fantasy he "escorts them home".'

A uniformed policeman and policewoman came onto the platform. Jason looked relieved. Natalia had to remind herself he'd only been in the job a few months, he was barely twenty. But he'd carried himself with complete professionalism tonight. Rasheda would be proud of him.

'Go,' she said. 'Do your job.'

Epilogue

Natalia opened the front door to find Sunil and Araminda outside. Araminda was holding the handle of a baby carriage. Inside, Natalia could just make out the black tuft of hair of their sleeping baby son. Both parents beamed at her.

'We're not making too much noise, I hope,' she said. Behind her came another whoop and then laughter from the living room.

'Oh no,' Sunil assured her. 'We didn't hear a thing.'

'We have a present for Connor,' Araminda said, smiling, handing a bag to Natalia. She looked inside and saw a parcel wrapped in birthday paper.

'Thanks. Are you coming in?'

Sunil and Araminda exchanged glances. 'Today we're taking the baby out to the park. It's the first time.'

'He's looking so well.'

'It was just a virus. Mr Kitson says he has no damage at all.'

Dermot came up behind her. 'What's this?'

'You've just missed Sunil and Araminda. They're taking the baby out for the first time, but dropped off a present for Connor.'

'That baby's a born survivor. I can't be saying the same for my son. Mark's destroyed him twice on that new computer game, even one-handed.'

'That's mean of him. He should let him win.'

'He told me he'll let him win next time. The scores are getting more even anyway.'

They went into the living room. Mark, left arm still in a sling from the chipped elbow he'd sustained tackling Jack Riley to the floor, was sitting on the settee beside Connor in front of the game that was running on the telly, each with a control box in hand. Nuala was watching them, cheering first Mark, then Connor, on.

'How did you get on with booking our tickets?' Natalia asked, as she and Dermot sat at the dining table.

'All booked. We'll be off to Italy in September.'

'Wonderful.' They exchanged smiles. 'Uh oh, there's the doorbell again. That'll be Mick.'

'I'll go.'

Mick was Dermot's brother. He, his wife

and children were over from Ireland, and were joining them for the two families to spend the day out together on Connor's birthday.

Mark got up. 'I'll be off now, then,' he said. Natalia had asked him to get hold of some football memorabilia for Connor, and he'd brought it round that morning.

'Your arm not hurting too much?'

'It's OK. I've had worse sports injuries! That Jack Riley, what a piece of work.' He shook his head. 'If we hadn't caught him red-handed, I wouldn't have believed it.'

'Polly, the young woman who lost her necklace, has identified him as the man who called himself Fred. And Cliff confirmed that Jack's missing PDA was found at Mornington Crescent. He remembered because he was joking with me about the station and the game, and so it stuck in his mind. That's why he was so keen to cover up the fact that it had ever been lost. Of course none of that's admissible. But still there's plenty of evidence against him.'

'How's Donna?' Mark asked quickly, as the sounds of greetings grew louder as Dermot led his brother and family into the living room.

'I spoke to her on the phone last night. A

bit sore physically. And furious! But grateful that we got there in time.'

Mark made his farewells and left, and then Natalia was hugging Mick and his wife, Dervla, before going into the kitchen to turn on the kettle and start making drinks for everyone. She was waiting for the kettle to boil when the phone rang. She walked through to the vestibule in the hall and picked up the receiver.

'Natalia? It's Harika here, from the Turkish Centre.'

'Oh yes, hello.'

'I have some news for you. I have an address. For your ex-husband. He and your son are in London.'

This Large Print Book, for people
who cannot read normal print,
is published under the auspices of

THE ULVERSCROFT FOUNDATION